Shirley
Thank you so much I hope you enjoy He Said&He Said as much as I enjoyed writing !!!
Dennis Reed II

He Said…She Said

A novel by

Dennis L. Reed II

He Said She Said
Published by arrangement with the author.

Printing History
First Printing: July 2006

ISBN: 978-0-9727498-3-1

Printed in the United States of America

Dedications

This book was made possible because of two groups of people and without all of you I really don't think I could have done it.

First this book has been made possible because of Jesus. Without my belief in him and knowing that anything is possible through him, I may have failed. There were times I never thought the book would be finished and I would go to sleep and wake up with a new fresh thought and I know it was only him. To Mom and Dad, you are the reason I am here and also the reason the book was able to be written (smile). I love you two more than life and don't think I don't appreciate everything you have done for me. My sisters Tracey, Kellie, Danielle, Lareaka, and Chantal I love each of you and I really am blessed to be able to call ya'll my sisters. Robert, man I miss you so much not only are you my only brother but my best friend. When you left me a part of me died. I really miss being able to be together and do the things that brothers do. You are gone from this earth but not from my heart. I love you and I miss you.

The next group the kids, Justin my little man daddy is so proud of you its crazy. Jasmine, my little lady, I love you and I can't wait to be able to have you around all day every day. Cameron, my baby I wanted you so bad. I couldn't wait for you to get here. You are my little blessing and that's for real. Marcel, I say it all the time, I really love the big brother you that are. You are great with J and Cam and I love you for that. Donita I smile when I think of you, and I am just glad you're the mother you are because you do that well. Thanks for you support and just being here to see me through all of this craziness.

He Said…She Said

Chapter 1

*I*t had been a typical day at the agency, deadlines and cranky production artists. Sequoia Johnson was a Senior Creative Director at the Reed Advertising Agency, a prestigious Black owned agency in New York City. She was working on a project for Chrysler and had put in over 40 hours this week and it was only Wednesday! She was trying to wrap things up with Sandy, a production artist that Sequoia worked closely with on some of her projects. Sandy had been complaining all day. First it was Sequoia making too many changes, then it was menstrual cramps and now she was hungry.

"Sandy, why don't we wrap it up and regroup for tomorrow. I need this out the door by Friday morning. But thank you for another productive day," said Sequoia.

"Thanks Koi. I hate to be so cranky but you know how it is. I'll see you first thing tomorrow morning," said Sandy as she closed her station down.

It was killing Sequoia that she had to work with Sandy on this project anyway. She promised herself she was going to get better with this wire frame stuff, if it killed her. She sat back in her chair and looked at the New York skyline from her window. It was still breathtaking but it would never be the same to Sequoia without the Twin Towers.

She had worked so hard to get this position, this office. She realized though that success had not come without a price. She was twenty-nine, still not married and no children, much to her mother's dismay. Deborah Johnson was the only female judge sitting on the New York State Supreme Court. Her husband Sederick Johnson was a retired investment broker on Wall Street. Needless to say Sequoia had not seen many bad days.

Although the Johnson's had hopes that she would follow down one of their career paths, she chose to utilize the creativity that she had been blessed with and instead enrolled at the Center for Creative Studies in Detroit, Michigan, where she graduated with a degree in Graphic Design. She worked at the Reed Agency as an intern while she was in school on summer vacation and started as a production artist the day she graduated and had been there ever since. She worked through all the channels and bureaucracy of the agency until she was soon recognized as one of New York's best and her six-figure salary clarified that.

She jumped up when she remembered she was supposed to be meeting Kenyon for dinner. Kenyon Burnett was her boyfriend of 4 years. She had met him at a fundraiser for her Mom. He had worked with her father in his last years at the Johnson, Spinks and Jackson Investment Firm. They immediately hit it off and began dating. Her parents were pleased.

"Shit, he's gonna kill me." She said as she ran down the hall to the elevators. "Come on. Come on," she chided the elevators. Finally the doors opened and she hopped on and prayed no one stopped her descent. 24 floors later, she hopped out and ran for the parking structure. She dialed his cell number as she jumped in her E320, an early 30th birthday gift to herself. He answered with extreme attitude.

"Yeah Koi. Wait, don't tell me. You had a last minute deal and couldn't leave." Said Kenyon.

"Ken, don't trip. You know that's exactly what happened. This is nothing new baby. You know about the Chrysler project and I'm sorry but I just lost track of time." Said Koi as she sped to the restaurant.

"Well, I'm sitting here waiting as usual," said an agitated Kenyon as he hung up his cell.

"Damn him. I mean we've only been together for 4 years. I was doing the same shit when I met him. He knows how this shit works. I feel like the damn man in this relationship. I don't have a fit when his dinner meetings with clients run over, do I?

Hell no, because I have my own shit to deal with. I've been in this business since I was twenty. Almost 10 years and I cannot change my ways. How I work has made me a success and I don't need a man that is gonna try to hold me back."

It was no secret that Kenyon was ready to settle down and have a family. They discussed it all the time and Sequoia wanted to be a Mom and a wife but she knew that it required several sacrifices that she wasn't sure she was ready to make just yet.

"Don't get me wrong, I love Kenyon to death. He is most definitely my soul mate. I remember the first month that we were dating, we were always together and if we weren't together we were on the phone. I recall we spent several hundred dollars on our cell phone bills. He is really a good guy. Notice I said a good guy, not perfect. He has flaws. Yes, he is fine. I mean, really fine. He is Panamanian and Jamaican. A beautiful blend. His caramel chocolate skin is smooth as a baby's bottom. Standing at 6"2 his athletic build is pure perfection from his years of playing basketball. Beautiful white teeth, a smile to die for and hazel eyes. Gorgeous! And he's an educated brother with a degree in Business Finance from the historical black college Morehouse.

So of course all these attributes make him a bit more confident than the average brotha. Ok brotha is arrogant! But he has the right to be. I'm not intimidated because I can handle my own. I'm not a spook you know! But he can be a bit demanding at times. And we've had our problems with his "fan base." Sometimes I've found that he can be a bit too friendly or anxious to help out a damsel in distress. I ain't insecure but I still don't need my man spreading himself all over the city."

Sequoia pulled up in front of the Tao restaurant and let the valet take her car. They were regulars, so the maitre' de kissed her cheek and guided her to their table were Kenyon was now entertaining two females. Sequoia walked up and Kenyon rose from his chair and introduced his "company."

"Sequoia Johnson this is Katy and Shanice. You remember Katy from the last company party and Shanice is the newest Administrative Assistant at the firm. They just so happened to be having an after work cocktail so I invited them to chill with me while I waited on you."

"Really? It's nice to meet you both. Thanks for keeping him company," said Sequoia as she took her seat. She waved the waiter over and Kenyon ordered a bottle of her favorite Merlot. Sequoia waited politely through a glass of wine and fifteen minutes of conversation before the two women left.

"Glad you could make it Koi," said Kenyon sarcastically.

"Oh! Now I'm Koi. Twenty minutes ago I was Sequoia Johnson, an associate of yours," said Sequoia.

"I did not say you were an associate. I was just being professional."

"Ain't that a bitch? The three of you didn't look like you were having a professional conversation when I walked up," said Sequoia.

"Can you lower your voice?" asked Kenyon as he noticed the neighboring tables turning to see what the racket was.

"I can do better than that. I'll see your ass at home. We do still live together don't we?" she said as she pushed her chair back.

Kenyon shook his head and poured another glass of wine as he watched his woman walk out the door.

He Said…

"Damn! I thought to myself I have to deal with this shit again. First she's late, then she storms out on me, but it's cool, it's all worth it I mean having a woman like Sequoia in my life makes my days a lot brighter and my nights a lot happier. Plus her attitude is exactly what I need to keep me in check. I know how I can be. I mean I have my fair share of "friends" but none of them are even on Koi's level.

I remember when I first met Koi her Dad invited my father and I to a fundraiser for Mrs. Johnson and I swear when I first saw Koi I swore to myself that I was going to marry her. Koi was 5'6, 130 pounds with a beautiful butterscotch complexion. She was often compared to Halle Berry. She was also blessed with a beautiful grade of hair, long and light brown with blond highlights. Though my favorite part of her body was her eyes. When I saw her I wanted to lick every one of her curves and I promised myself that if I ever had this woman as my own I would make her the happiest woman in the world.

"On the ride home I thought about what I could say to put a smile on my woman's face because ok, honestly I really messed up by introducing her the way I did but that's just how I am. It's not that I wanted either of the women at the table it's just that I guess I liked them liking me if you know what I mean. It makes a brotha feel good to be wanted. Koi should already know that I wouldn't even risk my job nonetheless our relationship on some office hoes. That ain't even my style."

While in deep thought about how I was going to make it up to Koi my cell rung and without looking at the caller id I answered the phone, "Hello?"

"Damn who killed your dog?"

"My fault frat, Sequoia and I got into a big one yo and I have to do something to make it up to her."

"Buy her some flowers that always works."

"I have to come better than some damn flowers but I'll come up with something. But let your mans think Colin I'll holla at you in a few."

"Well get at me tomorrow so we can hit the gym or something."

"Alright C. I'll holla at you after my 1 o'clock meeting."

"Alright one."

Colin was cool but he was always kind of corny when it came to women. I did flowers in college; with a woman like Koi you have to be up on your game. You have to really put some thought into any gift you get her and since this is a make up gift I know I'm really gonna to have to be on top of my game now. So on the way home I stopped at this little chocolate shop we used to go to the first month we met. And this is where the games begin.

She Said…

As soon as Koi was settled into their spacious loft apartment, she poured another glass of Merlot from the wine cooler that her best friend Nika had given her for Christmas. She flopped on the couch and flicked on the television. She actually hated TV and referred to it as the idiot box. She flipped through the 999 channels that were on Direct TV and found nothing of interest.

She tried listening to her newest CD by Floetry. That was relaxing enough. She checked their voicemail two calls from her Mom, one call Nika. She dialed Nika first.

"What's happening?" asked Sequoia.

"Ok, why did I meet P Diddy today? Ok maybe I didn't actually meet him but I came so close to meeting him." Said an excited Nika.

"How did this happen Nika?" Sequoia feigned excitement.

"I was at Justin's and he came in while we were eating lunch and his entourage walked past our table!"

"Nika, how do you get almost meeting him from that?" asked Sequoia.

Nika is what most men may refer to as a gold digger. But she's my homie though. She likes the good life and is usually willing to do whatever she has to do to acquire it. Her ultimate goal two years ago was to snag Kobe Bryant of the Los Angeles Lakers but that was blown out of the water when he married that little Latino girlfriend of his. I'm really not sure who she has set her sights on lately but she knows like I know that Puffy is out of arms length. Kim Porter ain't having no more J-Lo's raining on her Puffy parade. But anyway Nika won't stop at anything once she sets her sights so watch out Kim P.

Nika went on to explain that she slipped her number into his sports coat pocket when he walked by.

"You are crazy! You better be lucky one of his bodyguards didn't chop your hand off," said Sequoia.

"I'm smooth like that Koi. Your girl ain't new to this!" said Nika. "Hold on let me see who this is calling me."

Nika clicked over and Sequoia picked her nail while she waited for Nika to click back over. She silently wondered where Ken was. Nika clicked back over and told me it was her "Boo" so she would call me back. I didn't even ask who her "Boo" was because she called them all "Boo" so she didn't get them mixed up. That was her game and it worked.

Sequoia decided she needed a release. She changed into her work out clothes and jumped on the treadmill. She put Jay-Z's CD in her headset and went to work. She didn't hear Kenyon come in twenty minutes later. He had gone upstairs and was in the bathroom in their bedroom when she finally finished torturing her body.

When she noticed that he was home she prepared herself for round two. She knew that Ken was pissed because she had left the restaurant. He wasn't big on public confrontation and she knew it. But she knew she wasn't wrong for being upset about the scene she happened to walk in on. Okay granted she was wrong as two left shoes for being late in the first place but so what! They had trust issues on his part stemming from a few "mistakes" that he had made in the earlier part of their relationship.

"There was this one chick named Bianca. I swear whenever I find out who she is, her ass is done! She obviously didn't give a damn about the fact that he had a woman. How do you compete with a stank hoe that has no morals? So that was obviously a "mistake" that took a while for us to work through. And I'm not just going to sit around and end up going through that shit again."

Sequoia was ready to pounce all over him for the shit that had gone down. So of course she was surprised to see Kenyon running the Jacuzzi with bubbles and a plate of fresh chocolate dipped strawberries on the side. He had lit 4 votive candles in her favorite scent, jasmine. All the adrenaline and animosity that she had built up immediately vanished. She tried to apologize but he stopped her words with a kiss. They helped each other undress and slipped into the Jacuzzi. No words were spoken for about three minutes as they reconfirmed their love for one another through kisses. "Baby, I'm sorry for storming out on you but you know how I am." said Sequoia.

"Baby I didn't mean to make you feel uncomfortable when I introduced you. I called myself being professional but maybe I forgot to include the intimacy that we share in that introduction. But you know I was mad because I'd been waiting on you for an hour so I must admit it may have been intentional," explained Kenyon. "So let's call this one a truce."

"Yeah, we can do that for this one but you know I was salty as hell. You did a good thing, coming with the strawberries cause you were destined for the couch!" said Sequoia as she put a handful of bubbles on his nose.

"Don't even sweat that shit baby. Koi, you know you're my everything. I need and love you. Without you I don't know what I would do or where I would be. You honestly give me the strength to want more for the both of us and I want to give you everything because you deserve everything and I won't rest until I know I've given you the world and all the love in my heart."

Sequoia straddled him and kissed his forehead, then his nose and settled on his lips. Kenyon reached under the water and helped her and they made mad make-up love until the candles burned low.

"That's the other reason why I love this man so much. Brotha is the bomb in bed! I shudder to think where he picked up these skills. He has told me plenty of stories about his college days and the wild and crazy frat parties that they threw! I told you my man is fine and he was the star of the basketball team. You know they were on his shit. So I'm sure he is way more experienced than I am. When you can still name all of your lovers, it's safe to assume there haven't been many. But I'm not ashamed to say that he has taught me a lot. Am I wrong for wanting it all to myself?"

Sequoia rolled over at 6:30 and Kenyon was already up and running. She smelled a fresh pot of coffee brewing and once again thanked the Lord for her man. She showered and pulled a suit from her walk in closet. She barely missed Kenyon running out of the kitchen. He kissed her and yelled over his shoulder "I love you" as he raised the door to the freight elevator that opened in their foyer.

Sequoia was in the middle of swallowing a mouth full of coffee and mumbled "I love you too." She was actually minutes behind him because she wanted to make it to the office early to get started on the dreaded Chrysler project. She noticed his Range Rover was still parked in the structure when she walked out, which was weird. She assumed he had been picked up.

On her way to work she did the usual, people watching and dodging the crazy cabs that were darting in and out of traffic at will. She pulled into her parking space at 8:00 exactly.

The Reed Agency was housed in the Millender Building in midtown Manhattan. It was one of the largest black owned agencies in the country and Richard Reed the owner had built it from nothing. He had worked at two of the biggest agencies in

9

Michigan and one in Chicago before he realized that he needed to start his own agency. He built the Reed agency with tooth and nail and made it one of the best multi-cultural and diversified agencies around. They serviced some major accounts and lots of Fortune 500 companies. Sequoia was proud to be a part of it and she made sure she showed in every project her team sent out. Her production team had earned many prestigious awards for the work they had produced under her direction.

She was the first one in the office, as usual and was going over the other projects she had to assign when she was scared out of her wits by Richard Reed, himself.

"Good morning Sequoia. Nice to see you in here so bright and early. I wanted to let you know that I appreciate the loyalty and dedication that you exude to this agency and I have a project in my hands now that needs to done by the best. And you Sequoia are the best that I have and if this works out you stand to take a 6% commission from this multi-million dollar deal."

He went on to explain that a major athletic shoe store was about to change their whole brand identity and they had asked the Reed Agency to take on the design, marketing and execution of the project. He informed her that she had three weeks to come up with the comps. With that he shook her hand and walked out of her office like he had just stopped in to say hello, not like he had just dropped a major bombshell in her lap!

Sequoia quietly closed her door and covered her mouth and screamed with pure joy!! She reached for her phone and dialed Ken. She got his voicemail; she left a detailed message explaining it all and asked him to call her back ASAP!!

"I'm about to blow up baby!!" said Sequoia as she danced around her office.

Chapter 2

He Said…

See one thing I know for certain is Koi is a sucker for romance and in the romance department I'm the best and last night was no exception. When I walked in and saw my baby working out, I knew that I was either about to have a night to remember or a night on the couch and I'd much rather have the night to remember. Please believe, not to brag on myself but the strawberries, wine, candles, and the Jacuzzi all came totally natural and I used it to my full advantage.

The other thing I use to my advantage is Sequoia's lack of experience. See she's never had a sex partner like me. I mean, I was the first man to make her feel the way all her friends had bragged about. Before me she'd only had one guy taste her love and from her own admission, he didn't know what the hell he was doing. But when she encountered a brother like me that won't stop licking until she is shaking in ecstasy, she was sprung. And I'm still not happy until she tells me that she can't take any more and begs me to penetrate her love. I know I'm the bomb and I wasn't going to be happy until I made her forget whatever it was that was making her mad.

The next morning I woke up with an extra bounce in my step. I'd made love to my future wife and had a good nights rest. I would have never thought that my morning was going to be so fucked up.

After I got dressed and made a pot of coffee, I checked my two way and noticed I had a little less than a hour to get to the office to prepare for a meeting with a new VIP client. She wanted me to invest $4,000,000 on her behalf through J S & J.

The commission from this deal would give me enough to get that beach house in Jamaica, Koi wanted and I knew that would be the best Birthday present in the world for my baby and nothing was too good for her.

After giving Koi a kiss and leaving I went down to my truck and got in to start it up and it wouldn't start. I'm thinking to myself "What the fuck?" And then I saw the note on my windshield.

The note read: "Dear Kenyon, I'm sick of calling you and you're not returning my calls or my pages. You're not going to play me like some cheap hoe. So either you can contact me or I will contact your woman and I know you don't want me to do that. Oh and by the way I put a pound of sugar in your tank so your ass should know I'm not playing with you mutha fucka! So you better call me soon …Kim."

"Damn! I knew that I couldn't tell Koi so I just ran downstairs and had the doorman hail me a taxi. Note to self: Deal with Kim's silly ass later and call the dealer to pick up the Range after my meeting.

I got to the office a little before nine and had an hour to prepare for my meeting with Ms. Tanisha Roberts. She was a 35 year old from Montana who had just recently divorced one of the New York Knicks. She had received ten million in the settlement and was looking for a good investment. So Tanisha wanted me to work my magic with her money and I planned on doing it.

The hour went by so fast that I was surprised when my secretary buzzed me to let me know she was here. I told her to show her in. In walked a 5'8 Dark skinned, thin woman with jet-black hair that came past her shoulders. You could tell she was mixed with Indian or something. She was gorgeous but that wasn't what we were meeting for and I tried to stay focused.

We shook hands and made our introductions.

"Hello I'm Kenyon Burnett and you must be..."

Before I could get it out she said, "I'm Tanisha Roberts. Pleased to meet you. I see my girl wasn't lying. You are one fine gentleman. Maybe I should be trying to invest in you?" she said with a grin.

Playing her off like I really didn't hear her I said, "Well let's get to work." After an hour of explaining to her the market and IRA's we wrapped things up. It was still early in the day and I had to call to have the truck picked up before Koi got home. She always found a way to find her way home around lunch and it wasn't because she was hungry. She just did it to make sure I wasn't there with another woman and I couldn't blame her. I mean I've been caught a time or two and the trust issue was there but I was working on it.

Oh, and before I forget I need to call stupid ass Kim before she ends up at the apartment pushing every button to find out which apartment was mine, not knowing I'm in the penthouse. As I was calling the dealer my secretary buzzed me again and said there was a Kim here to see me. I told her to send her in. Before we hung up I told her to call the Range Rover dealer to have my truck picked up for service.

Kim walked in like nothing had happened. "Hey baby," she said as she took a seat on the edge of my desk.

"Hey baby? Man what the fuck is wrong with you? How the hell did you get in my parking garage and what's the deal with the sugar in my damn tank I swear!"

"You swear what? I've been fucking you for 4 months and you think I'm going to let you just leave me alone? You got me fucked up, Ken."

"I what? Bitch look, if you come around me again I will call the police. If you call me again, I will call the police and you better not come to my home again or I will beat your ass. Now get the hell out of here before I call security."

"Fuck you Ken."

"Kim, it's over between us. It was just a fling, you knew about my situation. Now get the fuck out."

"Just like that huh?" said Kim as she walked to the door.

"Yeah, just like that."

13

I called my secretary and told her to go on to lunch. She told me that Koi had called while I was in my meeting and the dealer had called back and told her that they'd picked up the truck. I thanked her and sat back and thought about what the hell I was going to tell Koi about the truck and why I didn't drive to work.

Well after an hour or so of sitting there wallowing in self-pity, I was surprised yet again when Koi walked in my office. "Hey Miss what you doing here?" I said with a surprised look on my face.

"I came to see my fine ass man, have you seen him?"

"Damn, I hope I'm that brotha. Come give your sexy man a kiss."

"A kiss? I had a little more in mind than just a kiss," Koi said with her right hand on her hip.

"So what do you have in mind?"

"Well baby I want to celebrate!" she said with a hint of attitude.

"Celebrate? Celebrate what baby?"

"You didn't get my message?"

"No I haven't checked my messages yet."

"Well check you cell phone Ken."

"Okay. What am I listening for?"

"Ken!" She said whining like a baby. "Mr. Reed gave me a huge project with an athletic shoe company and he said it's a multi-million dollar deal and your baby gets 6% of that! So you tell me, who's the woman?"

She was screaming so loud in my office and dancing around like a girl who had just got her first pair of diamond earrings. Even though I was happy about the good fortune for my baby, I knew that it also meant I would be seeing a lot less of the woman I love. And like my mom always said "Idle time is a devils workshop." And time is one thing I didn't need or really want while I was trying to be a one-woman man. That was hard enough without extra time to meet new friends if you know what I mean. But I wasn't trying to rain on my baby's parade.

I walked up to her and kissed her. She kissed me back and let me lift her onto my desk. As she laid back she pushed the papers I was working on to the floor. I unbuttoned her blouse and flipped her heels off and removed her thigh-high's. As I let my pants fall to my ankles I started having these crazy visions. It's like I was kissing Koi but I was seeing Kim. I shook my head in an effort to thwart those crazy ass thoughts. I kissed her breast and listened to her moan. I pulled her hips closer to the edge of the desk and inserted myself. I started to slowly please her and the visions were gone. I knew she was in the mood for a quickie so I pushed harder adding more energy to my thrust. She moaned uncontrollably. The heat I was feeling, plus the wetness and the tightness was driving me crazy. Hearing her moan was pushing me to the point where I couldn't control it anymore. She was begging me to come as I picked her up off the desk and used my strength to hold her in the air as I thrust deeper into her. She almost screamed as I came and called out "Kim."

She Said…

Ken was doing the damn thing to me as usual. I wasn't quite expecting the full Monty like I was getting. I had actually come to his office to give him oral pleasure. After last night I was still craving his body. On top of the good news Mr. Reed had delivered, shit I was straight up horny!

I was loving that shit and I started begging him to come because you know that hurt-so-good feeling? Well it was starting to hurt-so-much. He was killing me. Then when he came, I heard him say my name but it kind of sounded like he said something else. I was still in the air and he was still shaking and moaning after he had released so I didn't want to spoil it by asking him what he said. I'm tripping I thought to myself. This Negro loves me.

He lifted me up and off and put me back down. We started gathering our clothes from on the floor. I used his Executive bathroom to rinse off and got dressed. When I came out he was still shirtless but he was on the phone. I kissed him and mouthed that I would see him later and to call me.

As I rode the elevator down, I replayed the scene in my head and tried recall what Ken had said but I still couldn't get it. Let me stop tripping I said again. I forgot to ask him what was wrong with the truck this morning. Oh well, I'll talk to him later.

Chapter 3

*W*hen I got back to the agency, Sandy was hard at work on the wire frame project and it was looking good. I didn't bother her. I went to check on some of the other projects in house. Jeff, a retoucher was working on some print ads for a fashion magazine. You'd be surprised to find that all the models that you see aren't as beautiful as you think. A lot of retouching is done to make them perfect like they are when the magazine hits the stands.

Karl was doing a web design for a pharmaceutical company. This guy was a genius. He had no degree, all self taught but he could hang with the big boys. I was lining up all my ducks in a row because we had to put some good shit together for this new project.

I stood at the edge of the production room and looked over all my "teammates." I definitely had some talented people working with me and I was pumped and ready to get started. I figured I would announce the project on Friday so that I could get them motivated and they would be refreshed and ready on Monday.

When I got back to my office, my extension was ringing. I answered but no one was on the line. I rang the receptionist and asked her who she had just patched through. She said it was a woman but she hadn't given her name. That's funny, I thought. It must have been Nika, she'll call back.

The day sped by like lightening. I was focused but I made sure that I was out of there at 5:30 and at home by 6:00, much to Ken's surprise. The truth is I was worn out from this afternoon's quickie session and I could barely keep my eyes open.

But I was reenergized when I saw my baby lying on the couch, when I pulled the elevator door up.

I really love this man. My parents love this man. He is probably every parents dream son-in-law. My father had taken him under his wing and showed him all that he knew. My mother was thrilled when we started dating because she was so afraid that I was going to settle down with a starving artist type. Like I had room to judge. I had refused any financial help from my parents, other than tuition when I was in school. I was the true definition of a starving artist. I waitressed at an Italian restaurant in downtown Detroit called *Intermezzo* to pay my studio apartment rent. I ate so much Italian food that I don't even like to look at pasta now.

So needless to say, when Ken and I hit it off they both were ecstatic. My Mom was always dropping hints about grandbabies and my father had already told Ken they set money aside for my wedding.

I cooked up a pot of stir-fry vegetables with rice and set the table. Kenyon was watching a basketball game so I brought his plate to him in the den. I had cracked a fresh bottle of Chianti and poured him a glass. He mumbled a thank you and continued watching the game. He had his laptop open on the table so I assumed during commercials he was working.

Okay, so I'm home early for the first time in months and where do I fit in this scenario. So I watch the Kings kick the Mavs butt for minute. After he puts his plate on table I try to sit on his lap but he is just about to pick up his laptop so it jabs me in the thigh.

"Ouch!"

"Sorry baby"

"What's up Ken? I'm here early and you haven't said two words to me. I thought this is what you wanted."

"It is. I'm sorry baby but I'm just trying to get some things in order for this new client. I'll be done in a minute."

I'm like "whatever" as I pick up our plates and drop them in the dishwasher. I start to go back into the den with him but think twice about it and instead decide to finish my latest fictional novel by M. Bridges. It's been sitting on my nightstand for months.

I can't concentrate so I turn on the CD player with the remote. He was listening to Blu Cantrell's latest joint last. It's jazzy so I like it. I am bored to death. I could've been at work, actually working on the million things I have to do.

I call Nika to see what she is up to.

"What are you doing?" I ask.

"It," she replies.

"What do you mean it?" I ask.

"It girl. I'm doing it," she says as I hear rustling and a distant moan in the background.

"Oops! My bad. Call me later," I say as I hang up the phone with a giggle.

I open some packs of pictures that I've been meaning to put in the photo albums and thumb through them. I laugh at one of me and Nika at a Hair Show this past summer. The next pack is filled with pictures of me and Ken in Detroit when we went to visit my girl Sydni. She owns a bar in the city and we met through a mutual friend Chyna, who lives in Chicago. I swear when we all get together it's a hoot.

Speaking of Chicago, I get salty instantly when I see the pack of pictures that Ken and his frat brothers took when they went to the Taste fest together. That would be when he fucked around with Bianca. I close that pack up and decide this project can wait a few more months.

That was probably the worst time in our relationship. I remember his phone ringing at 3:00 in the morning, minutes after he had stumbled in the house too drunk to take his clothes off. I answered thinking it was one of his frats making sure his drunk ass made it home. Instead it was Bianca.

"Hello?"

"Why are you answering his phone?" asked Bianca.

"Excuse me? Who the hell is this?" I asked, fury building by the minute.

"That's really none of your business," she replied.

"See that's where you're wrong. It is my business. And I want to know who you are and why the fuck you are calling my man at 3:00 in the morning."

"Well actually I'm returning "your man's" call. I assume he's in for the night so I'll just try him back tomorrow," she said and hung up the phone.

I was so mad but I gathered my thoughts and searched through his phone for his most recently dialed calls. Sure enough, he had placed a call at 2:48. I pressed send and called the number back. The wench must have turned her phone off because my call went straight to her voicemail: Hi this is Bianca. Please leave me a message and I will gladly return your call.

"Look bitch, you obviously know about me so this makes you as guilty as he is. You must realize that you are nothing but a piece of ass to him. You could never be wifey material because he wouldn't be calling your hoe ass at 2:45 in the morning. You do know that's called a booty call right? So if you are satisfied with being a hoe then so be it, but don't ever let me find out who you are, sleaze."

I snapped out of that daydream/nightmare and suddenly felt ill. I went to the bathroom to throw up. The same bathroom that had been the scene of beautiful love making the night before.

I was disgusted. I hated when I thought about that old shit. It made me hate him. I was so humiliated after all that. Here I am working my ass off all day, coming home making sure I make love to him and doing whatever I thought it was that made him happy but that wasn't enough for him. He had to go and fuck with some hoe that didn't mind that he had a woman. It still made me sick. And now here he is acting funny all over again. I pray that he is not fucking around because honestly I can't take it anymore. My imagination is so vivid. For months after that I wouldn't let him sleep in the bed with me because I constantly saw him fucking this mystery woman in my mind.

Nika told me that was the biggest mistake. If I wasn't fucking him then he was probably still fucking her. But I couldn't bring myself to do it and I couldn't bring myself to let him go. Please Lord don't let this happen again.

I finished vomiting and cleaned myself up. I went back into the kitchen to get a glass of water and noticed Kenyon was gone. He didn't even tell me he was leaving. I put my pajamas on and started reading my book. I fell asleep with the book on my face. When I woke up to turn light out I looked at the clock, ironically it read 2:48 a.m. and Ken was not at home.

He Said…

Hell yea!! My team finally beat the punk ass Mavs. I loved Philly because Chris Weber played for them and he was one of the Fab Five at the University of Michigan. I think anyone that played basketball in the 90's loved the Fab Five.

While I was watching the game I was working on Ms. Robert's portfolio when my two way started vibrating. Oh shit, I thought to myself. I thought I had cut this thing off. I started doing that when Koi kept catching me. When I read the message it said, "Urgent call Colin @718-555-3632". When I grabbed my cell to call Colin back I instantly got his voicemail, but while I was leaving him a message he beeped in on my cell so when I clicked over Colin started ranting and raving like he was crazy!

"Colin. Colin! Calm down what's going on?"

"Man I can't believe this shit! I'm about to kill this bitch!!!"

"What bitch?"

"Chanelle!"

"For what C?"

"Man I came over her crib to surprise her with some flowers, you know trying to put a little romance in our relationship and this bitch is in there sucking your boy Mark's dick."

"What?" I said trying my best to hold in my laugh. "Man where you at?"

"Ken I'm sitting outside this bitch's house!"

"Man what are you about to do?" I said with a little concern in my voice.

"I'm about to kill this bitch and your punk ass friend!" Colin said trying to hold back his tears so I wouldn't think he was soft.

"I'm on my way so calm down dude and don't do anything until I get there. Okay?"

"Yeah well you better hurry up because I'm mad as hell and I'm ready to fuck somebody up! You know where Chanelle lives right?"

I wanted to tell him everybody knew where she lived but instead I answered "Yeah, up town off White Plains right?"

"Yeah I'll be outside."

"Okay yo. Be safe and don't do shit until I get there...one."

"Okay ... one."

Damn I had to hurry up to Colin because he was one of those quiet types that you thought wouldn't hurt a fly but when he got mad, everybody better watch out. I remember in college he caught a case because he beat a boy up so bad. Luckily he only got probation. But I understood his anger this time but I'd tried to warn him.

His girl Chanelle was a hoe and everybody knew it but him. I had told him before to stop bringing her around to the hangouts and events where it was just supposed to be "the boys." But he wouldn't listen. I mean, your boys are your boys but it's something about the temptation of the forbidden fruit. I knew

22

something was going down with Mark and Chanelle but I didn't say anything because Colin was so sprung that he wouldn't have believed it anyway.

I sped along Lennox Ave thinking all along I better hurry back because Koi couldn't stand Colin and if she knew I was going to help him she would have really gone off because I was using her car. But she would have done the same for Nika. I can't stand that sack-chasing ass Nika. You talk about a hoe! If you look hoe up in the dictionary her picture is right under the word. I must give the hoe her props though. She had definitely laid down with some of New York's big wigs from politics, to sports, right on down to hip-hop. The girl gets around. I hate for her and Koi to go out together because I know that niggas think, "Birds of a feather flock together." And I don't want them thinking my baby is some kind of tramp. But that's her girl and if she needed her for any reason she would go. So I'll just deal with her attitude later when I get back.

When I pulled up in front of Chanelle's house where I'd been countless times before she and Colin had started dating, Colin was parked in front looking war torn and destitute.

I got out of the car and knocked on his window. He jumped out and said "You ready to do this?"

"Man we ain't about to do nothing. I came here to get you and pull you away from this madness. I tried to tell your ass before that messing with her was a bad idea. This is what she does man. She doesn't want to settle down."

"Look Ken, either you're down with me or you're against me."

"Colin I know you aren't raising up on me. I'm your man. I'm trying to help your ass do the right thing. This hoe ain't worth you violating your probation. Plus how do you know she's sucking his dick?" I asked half curious and wanting to see for myself. She had the bomb head game.

"I have a key, asshole. I walked in on the shit but they didn't see me."

"See so you thought better of it anyway. You wouldn't have turned around if you wanted to do something." I said trying to convince him that he was the bigger man.

"Yeah, I guess so. But man your boy is scandalous." Said a dejected Colin.

"Yeah, I guess but he isn't committed to you, she is. So if you're mad at anybody it should be her. But you need to deal with her ass later. Come on, let's go grab a brew."

Colin conceded and got back in his car. As I led him to the nearest watering hole I could find, I thought about my own relationship. I had basically ignored Koi when she came home today. Not intentionally but I wanted to take care of that account so that I can give her the best. With the draw I'm gonna get for the Roberts account, I'm really gonna be able to take this thing to another level. I had already been to Tiffany's and scoped out a few rings. I knew that her favorite was the Princess cut. I was finally going to be able to show her that I really appreciate her hanging in there through all my bullshit. But first I had to stop my friend from committing a lethal mistake.

She Said…

I'm so mad right now. I can't believe this asshole just climbed into the bed and kissed me. Smelling like a fifth of Jack Daniels at that! When I heard the elevator door I looked at the clock. 4:15 it read. I'm pissed. I move his arm from around my waist because right this very minute I really want to slap the hell out of him! I try to go back to sleep but I can't because his drunk ass is snoring so damn loud. I snatch the cover off the bed and my pillow and leave his ass shivering in the middle of the bed and go to the couch. I lie awake thinking of ways to torture my man. I decide on silence. That always works. I finally doze off fifteen minutes before my alarm goes off! Damn!

I get up and shower and don't wake him up. I'm sure he has some sort of meeting this morning but it would require me to speak to him to wake him up. I put on a fresh pot of coffee because judging from his breath he is gonna need it. I get in my car and am instantly even more pissed than I was before. This Negro used a 1/2 tank of gas last night!! Where the hell did he go? Oooohh! I'm pissed.

When I get to the agency, Mr. Reed is already seated in my office with another gentleman. I immediately touch my hair, which I pulled back in a ponytail because I was too tired to do anything else to it and curse myself for wearing khakis today.

"Good morning gentlemen," I say as I hang my coat up and try not to look surprised.

"Good morning Sequoia. I'd like to introduce Mr. De'Rico Matthews, a premier graphic designer that I've been in talks with. I'd like you to look over his portfolio and let me know what you think. I value your opinion Sequoia. De'Rico may be someone that you can use on this new project," Mr. Reed said with a wink.

I suddenly felt like no matter what I thought, Mr. Matthews was in. But as I thumbed through his portfolio, I was truly impressed. I actually felt that he would definitely be an asset to the project. His ideas were new and fresh and I saw a lot of myself in him. I gave Mr. Reed my opinion and waited for further direction. He informed me that Mr. Matthews had been freelancing and was available immediately. Mr. Reed left us to chat a bit and asked me to walk him back up to his office when we were done.

I then realized why I had been so self-conscious when I walked in my office. De'Rico was fine. He stood at an even 6 feet. I estimated him to be about 205. He was chocolate brown with shoulder length dreads. He was dressed in washed out jeans with an off white linen shirt.

I invited him to have a seat at the conference table in my office. We talked about his experience and the work that he had showcased for Mr. Reed and myself. I told him about the project and he was genuinely interested and excited about it. He was also excited about working under my direction. He told me that I had earned a stellar reputation in the advertising community and he was thrilled to even get to meet me. I decided at that moment that I wanted him on my team.

I introduced him to the other team members and noticed a new sparkle in Sandy's eye. Oh Lord! I thought to myself. I showed him some of the ad campaigns we had done. I gave him a desk and had the receptionist set him up a line. I told him he was welcome to start on Monday but he insisted on starting today, which was cool because I still had that wire frame to get out for Chrysler today. And of course Sandy was thrilled to be working with him anyway. This freed me up for a minute to work on some other projects.

I was doing some copywriting for a brochure for a construction company that we were doing work for when De'Rico invited me to lunch. I really needed to finish what I was working on but I decided to go ahead anyway. I grabbed my purse and off we went.

Chapter 4

He Said…

*N*ooooooooo!!!! I peeked over at the clock, which read 9:20 a.m. I am so late and my head is banging. "Koi! Koi! Baby where are you?" No answer. I thought to myself, she must be at work. But why she didn't wake me up and how the hell did I get home? The last thing I remember was drinking with Colin and telling him he was lucky that he found out about Chanelle before the bitch got pregnant or she tricked his silly ass into marrying her. The next thing I know I'm in my bed cold as hell, without a cover and a banging ass headache.

I got out of bed smelling some freshly brewed coffee I was never a real coffee drinker but Koi was so I would get up every morning and make a pot for her. But this morning I found myself savoring a cup while I was getting dress and drinking another on the way to work!

The unwelcome ringing of my cell phone only made my head pound even harder.

"Hello," I said praying that the two Advil I'd taken would stop my head from pounding.

"Ken I need to talk to you."

"What's wrong Janee?"

"Mom is tripping. She's still having reservations about me going away to school. Please talk to her for me Ken. You have to get through to her. I want to move to the ATL so bad. I worked so hard to get accepted to Spelman College. I don't want it to go down the drain, so please talk to her."

"Okay Janee. I'll talk to her as soon as I get to my office. Just relax. It'll all work out."

"Thank you so much. You're the best brother in the world."

"It's easy to be the best brother in the world, to the best sister in the world."

Janee was the youngest 3 children. But since my brother Lavon was killed in a car accident, our parents seemed to be over protective of Janee. I think it really bothered Janee because she was a really independent young lady and my parents were smothering her. She had wanted to go to Spelman since she was nine. Right after my mom took her down there for an Alpha Kappa Alpha Inc. Big Sister of America conference.

I got to the office around 11 and checked my messages. No message from Koi. I wasn't surprised. I decided to take her to lunch and then I could explain what happened last night. I finished the report that I had to have for my next meeting and then left to meet my queen.

I used the company limo and once I was settled in I called my mom, to talk to her about Janee going down to Atlanta. I knew it wasn't going to be easy. I just hoped I could get a word in edgewise because when my mother got started there was no stopping her. Especially about her baby. I really wanted Janee to go to Spelman because not only was it a great school but it had a history of great woman who had studied there including my Mom.

My mom was the first black president of Chase Bank, one of the top 5 banks in the world. She was very powerful and when she said something people listened, and our family was no exception.

I tried my Mom's direct line but only got her voicemail. I left her a message to call me back as soon as she could. And I knew she would. It was rare that I called her at work. I hung up and called Koi to let her know I was coming by. I was around the corner but I knew she was there because she rarely took a lunch break.

The receptionist answered, "Thank you for calling the Reed Agency."

"Sequoia Johnson please."

"I'm sorry you just missed her. Would you like to leave a message?"

"Do you know where she went?" I asked a bit surprised that she was gone.

"She went to lunch. Would you like to leave a message?" asked the receptionist with a bit of an attitude.

I still hadn't instructed the driver differently so he still proceeded to the front of the Agency.

What I saw made me not only pissed but sick as hell. I saw my woman walking out the office building with this guy with dreads! He opened up her car door and got in on the other side. That pissed me off but instead of getting upset I played it cool.

"Tim," I called on the limo phone.

"Yes sir?"

"Follow that Benz right there."

"No problem sir," he replied.

As we followed Koi in her car, my anger intensified. That's when my game plan kicked in. I called her cell phone and was only even more pissed when the phone rang once and she sent me straight to voice mail. Luckily we had Nextel's so I radioed her. She didn't respond and when I tried again, she had turned the phone off. Suddenly I was feeling really sick. Who was this nigga with my woman and why won't she answer my call? I guess I'll find out soon enough. I'm gonna wait and watch and let her hang herself.

"I'm mad as hell."

She Said…

"I can't believe this Negro is trying to blow my phone up now," I thought to myself. "Now why the hell didn't he think to call last night? Just some typical "Old Ken" shit. I told his ass before, I'm not having that shit again." I turned my phone off. I didn't want to be embarrassed any more than I already was.

Fortunately Rico didn't mention that rude outburst from my phone. I'm starting to hate Nextel. Rico suggested Justin's on 132nd for lunch. That was cool. I thought of Nika and her near miss with P. Diddy and giggled.

"What's funny?" asked Rico.

I told him about Nika and how silly she was. He thought she was cool for being so ambitious. I thought about how much Ken hated her ways and the names that he called her.

Rico was truly a gentleman. He was opening car doors and pulling out chairs. It was really refreshing to know that chivalry wasn't dead. Mind you my man is a gentleman but sometimes he gets relaxed and I'll find myself sitting in the car while he is already walking up to the restaurant or wherever. But I guess that happens when the relationship gets old.

We were seated almost immediately. We didn't order for almost an hour because our conversation was so interesting. We found that we had a lot of mutual friends in the business. We finally ordered and nibbled at our food during the brief pauses in the conversation. Before we knew it we had been gone for well over two hours.

When we returned to the Agency I welcomed him on board and we discussed the Athletic Shoe deal in detail. We were brainstorming and feeding off of one another and had come up with a comp before we knew it. Sandy had finished the wire frame deal and I had our intern deliver it. My day had actually shaped up to be very productive despite the rocky start.

I checked my voicemail and noticed no messages from Ken. It was already 6 and I knew I had promised to work on the late evenings for Ken, but screw him I thought. I had work to do and why was I running home to him? To be ignored again? I don't think so.

I took off my jacket and stretched as I looked at the view from my office window. I kicked off my heels and walked barefoot to the break room for another cup of coffee. As usual everyone was already gone as I suspected. So of course I was almost shocked shitless when I entered the break room and saw Rico already there brewing a fresh pot.

"Oh my God! What are you doing here?" I asked suddenly feeling very self-conscious of my stocking feet.

"I'm sorry. I didn't mean to startle you. I usually stay a little longer than most of my co-workers. I've been told that's why I don't have a wife yet. When I saw the masses head for the hills at 5'o clock, I assumed it would be the same here," he said.

I noticed him looking at my feet. "Oh Lord I hope my French manicure hasn't cracked," I thought to myself.

"You are classy woman from head to toe, I see," said Rico. "Nothing better than a woman with pretty feet, and a head on her shoulders."

"Don't be talking about my feet now Rico. We just met," I found myself flirting back. It was hard not to. He was gorgeous. We waited together as the coffee maker slowly brewed the pot of java. I quickly found myself laughing again. He was hilarious.

We walked back to his station so he could show me some of the designs that he had been working on since lunch. Again I was impressed.

"I think we are going to make a great team, Ms. Johnson."

"I agree Mr. Matthews."

It was after 9 o'clock when I walked in the house. I slipped off my heels and put my briefcase down at the door as I thumbed through the mail that Kenyon must have set on the sofa table. I stretched and yawned and when I opened my eyes Ken was standing there, and he wasn't looking happy.

He Said…She Said

Chapter 5

He Said…

9 had been home since 6pm and all I could think about was Koi and her little lunch date. It's not like Koi to cheat but who was this man? He wasn't a family member and what made him so damn important she couldn't answer her phone?

I had decided to work out and let a little frustration out on the punching bag and lift a few weights. My hopes were that by the time Koi came home, I would be able to talk to her and keep my anger under control. I had never put my hands on a woman but for the first time in my life, I wasn't sure if I could maintain my composure. I wasn't used to not getting my way. And my woman cheating on me, made me feel less than a man. I promised myself I was going to get to the bottom of this shit as soon as she brought her ass home.

After my work out, I was in the bath soaking, reading *Second Time Shame on Me* by Erica N. Martin. She's a client of mine. I promised her I would read her book and much to my surprise it calmed me down. I was still pissed but I was willing to at least talk to her and see what was going on. I heard the elevator and wrapped a towel around my waist.

When I came into the foyer she was yawning and stretching like she was trying to recharge her battery from a long day of working or fucking.

"Hey Miss. What's going on? How was your day?"

Koi looked at me with a strange look and answered, "It was fine. Why do you ask?"

"What? Now I can't ask my woman how her day was? By the way, I stopped by to see if you wanted to go to lunch today but they said you were already gone."

"Well, maybe you should try calling first."

"Well maybe you should keep your phone on. You know Koi it's cool. I have a lot of work to do so I'm about to go back to the office. You know all about those late nights right? So if I was you I wouldn't wait up."

"I guess your ass was at the office last night too right?"

"Koi what are you talking about? Why don't you just ask me where I was, instead of assuming?"

"All I know is when I woke up my man was no where to be found. I don't know where you were, what you were doing, or who you were doing!"

"I guess I was doing the guy with the dreads wife."

"Ken what the hell are you talking bout? What guy with the dreads?"

"You know the guy you were at Justin's with."

"Ken he works with me." "

"Well why didn't you answer the phone?"

"Because …"

"Yeah I thought so. I'll talk to you later. Don't wait up."

"Ken, don't try to change this shit around. You stayed out all night and now you're trying to switch the blame over to me because I had a simple lunch with a co-worker."

"Don't wait up."

"I won't. Oh and by the way he doesn't have a wife."

On the way to the office all I could think about was why were we having so many problems. So this guy is a co-worker but then why she couldn't answer her phone?

When I had my mine set on one thing and that was to find out the truth about the guy with the dreads.

She Said…

After Kenyon left, I went to change into my pajamas. I could not believe he was trying to flip the script on me. But I wasn't falling for it, not this time. I changed and went to the kitchen and took out the pint of Häagen-Dazs ice cream. I put it back because that was comfort food and I was not going to let him reduce me to feeling guilty about anything.

It was going to be a long night. I was lying in bed thinking about Kenyon and how things had changed. I had just started feeling comfortable again with him. There were days when I thought he might be playing around again, but he always followed up with a day that made me feel like his queen. I just wasn't sure why all of a sudden he would do something stupid like stay out until the wee hours of the morning.

I know I am a beautiful woman and I tend to my man's needs. What would make a man cheat on someone that showed him unconditional love? There wasn't anything that we hadn't done together. I drew the line at a threesome, only because I couldn't bear to see him fucking someone else. I love Ken, sometimes too much. My love for him is so deep that there is no turning back. He has stepped all over my heart and I stayed.

Never once had I considered cheating on him. In the business I'm in, I encounter fine ass men all the time. Models for photo shoots, athletes, all kinds of men. But never once have I strayed. Ken was my partner, my friend. He had taught me so much.

So why was I thinking about Rico? I slid deeper into the pillow top mattress. As I envisioned De'Rico Matthews standing at the door to my office, I imagined him without his shirt on. I rubbed my breast thinking about him kissing me. I saw us at lunch, him wiping a crumb from my mouth and me sucking his finger. My hands wandered down my stomach. I imagined him climbing into my bed, butt booty naked and lying on top of me. My fingers began to massage the hidden pearl of ecstasy. I felt his warm body on top of mine and felt his hardness on my thigh. My body shuddered as I imagined him forcing his way into me, thrusting in and out. I saw his muscles flexing and felt his dreads hitting my face with each thrust. My body arched as I brought myself to an orgasm. I was drenched. Literally drenched. My silk gown was stuck to my body. My fingers were wet. I was breathing hard as hell. But I felt so good. My legs were shaking as I turned over on my stomach and thought about…what's his name? Oh yeah, Ken.

He Said…

When I arrived at my office, I was feeling really bad about how thing were going with Koi and I. I mean this is my future wife and here I am thinking about leaving. Koi is the mother of the child I dream of having. But every time I thought about Koi I kept seeing her and this guy sitting in Justin's and her looking into his eyes and not even answering her phone. I mean what was so damn important for her to ignore my calls?

Hours came and went and the more I thought about Koi I knew that I had to change my life for the woman that I love. What will it take for her to understand that she's my partner in life, my queen, my everything. I was thinking about all these changes when I saw a light beaming under my door.

Shanice, my new assistant was still in the office to my surprise. She was a cool girl and fine as hell. Shanice was 5'7, 125 pounds. I mean put together very well! She was Hispanic and every time she said my name I swear I would melt where ever I was standing. Since I also spoke Spanish fluently, we would often use sexual innuendos around the office, no one ever caught wind to what we were saying. She was educated at NYU and I swear having her on my team was good for business but not good for my hormones.

While I was sitting there in deep thought there was a knock at my door. "Who is it?" I asked surprised that anyone was even here with me.

"It's me, Shanice."

"Shanice." I said with mock surprise in my voice. I knew she was there working her ass off so she could make it seem like she knew her job inside and out during the day.

"Kenyon what are you doing here so late?"

"I was here just trying to get some of this work done for the Roberts file."

"Really I was just organizing your files. Can I pull one out for you? That is if it's safe. I wouldn't want your wife to show up and blow the spot up," she said trying to act like she really cared if I was married or not.

"Well first off, I'm not married and secondly my woman is at home sleep."

"Well I am sure if I get to close she will feel her leash yank. From the cold reception we got the other day at the bar, she seems like she can be a feisty one."

"Don't anybody have a leash on me, I'm a grown ass man but she does have lo jack on my ass so I better not say the wrong thing." I said it jokingly but I was dead serious. Koi wasn't that naïve young woman I knew before.

Shanice did that really cute giggle that I had learned to love.

"Well I am here to assist you. What do you want me to do?" she said.

As I looked at her standing there with her hands on her voluptuous hips, I wanted to say: I want to bend your ass over and make you call me Papi. But instead I said "Can you get me Tanisha Roberts file?"

"No problem, I'll be right back."

I quickly ran into my private bathroom and threw some water on my face and prayed whenever Shanice came back I would behave myself. That was going to be very hard if she kept licking her lips the way she had been doing ever since she walked into my office.

I looked up in the mirror and the only reflection I saw was Shanice standing butt naked with Mrs. Roberts' file and a smile. I couldn't help but stare. I wanted her so bad but I couldn't tell her that, but she knew by the man hood that had grown in my pants.

"Look Ken I don't want shit but to make you happy. I swear I will make you forget about whatever it is that is bothering you tonight."

I wanted to believe that. I guess that's why when she started kissing my neck I just melted on my desk and just embraced every little kiss and touch. She took off my shirt and kissed my chest. I held her tight like she was Koi and that was something I had never done before. Most women were just a fuck but this was much more. I took my time with Shanice. I laid her on the couch in the office and went straight to the center of her being. I showed her what a man can do when he is trying to make a woman his own. I knew I was making my point by the way she grabbed my head and told me, "I love you." That's when I knew I had to stop.

"Ken! What are you doing?" she said,

"Look Shanice, you don't even know me. Let's chill with the love shit."

"Ken I've loved you since the first time that I saw you."

"Well let's get one thing straight. I don't feel the same. Don't get me wrong, you are a great person but I'm in love with Sequoia. I should be home with her right now, not here with my head between your legs thinking about her."

"Look there's no need to trip. I only want a little of your time and affection. I'm not trying to break up your happy home. Go home think about it and if you just want me to be your girl on the side let me know."

From the look in her eyes, she meant it. She wanted me to be her man any way she could have me and if that meant her getting a piece of me once a month she would be content with that. Somehow it seemed like I'd heard this before.

"Look Shanice …" The phone stopped me before I could finish "Excuse me for a second, hello?"

"Hey baby," the voice said on the phone.

"Who is this?"

"It's your wife, mother fucka."

I immediately recognized the voice. It was Kim's crazy ass. Just what I needed, thought to myself.

"What the hell are you calling me for? Didn't I tell…"

"Tell me what mutha fucka? I told you shit ain't gonna go that easy. The sugar was just the beginning unless you regain your senses. You are my man."

"Kim look I'm in a meeting. I'll see you later." I said, barely able to contain my anger. This bitch was on my last nerve.

"Later?" she said shocked not knowing it was just a ploy to get her ass off the phone.

"Yeah Kim, later." We hung up and Shanice looked at me and with those sweet brown eyes and said "I see your ex is tripping.

"How do you know she's my ex?"

"I've been meaning to tell you to watch the company you keep because that broad is crazy. She's made it very clear when she calls that she is a VIP in your life. Luckily I can keep a secret. But now I want to be your little secret."

"Look Shanice, I have enough on my plate right now. I don't need anymore problems."

"Ken, all I want is for you to be happy. I won't ever nag or bother you. Handle your business. I'll see you in the morning." She gave me a peck on the cheek and left.

I sat there in my office for a few more minutes and thought about what had just happened and how I was going to handle Kim's dumb ass. I didn't need this shit happening right now because Koi and I are already going through some shit. I didn't need this bitch making things worse, so I wrapped up and headed straight to Kim.

On the way to her apartment, I thought about what I was going to say to her. I knew what ever I said had to work because I never wanted to hear her voice again. When I pulled up, I called her to come down.

When she got in the car she tried to give me a kiss.

"What the fuck is wrong with your girl? Why are you fucking with me Kim?"

"Ken you said you loved me and you wanted to be with me. Now all of a sudden you just quit me cold turkey. No calls, no visits or anything. What do you expect me to do?"

"Look, I never said that shit Kim. I know I hurt you, how can I make it better?"

"Fuck me nigga. That will make it better," she said defiantly.

"Kim, you know I can't do that. You can't handle it. I told your ass from the beginning that I wasn't leaving my woman and not to get attached."

"Well it can't get better then."

"Look I will pay you." I know y'all are laughing but I was desperate at this point.

"Nigga I got a job. I might not be some big shot ad agency or whatever she is, but I can hold my own. She must not be all that because if she was you would have never slipped into my bed."

When she said that I lost it. It was like I snapped. I started choking the life out of her. She was feeling the wrath for everything that had gone wrong that day.

"Bitch do you think I am playing with you? I will kill you. Don't fuck with me!"

Kim was tearing at my hands, trying to regain her freedom. "Ken please!!"

I let her go when I realized what I was doing. She was coughing trying to catch her breath. Gasping in and out trying to fill her lungs with the much needed air that I had denied her.

"Kim, please just leave me alone. I don't want you anymore. We kicked it for a minute. It was fun, but it's over. You are pathetic and I can't stand the sight of you. You need to spend some of this energy you are using chasing me around to get your life together."

I watched her as her breathing started to slow down and the tears had started, but I was careful not to let my guard down. Because she is crazy as a June-bug and I expected her to leap on me at any moment. Instead she got out of the car and said, "If that's how you want it, then fine. Good-bye Ken." She closed the car door and went back inside.

Now I was really fucked up. I didn't feel good about choking Kim but she was out of control and I didn't know what else to do. I mean this chick was relentless. The head was spectacular but I didn't want to fuck with her anymore. Why can't everyone see that I'm trying to straighten my life up?

He Said…She Said

Chapter 6

She Said…

I woke up totally refreshed from a good nights sleep. I wasn't even pissed that Kenyon didn't bring his ass home until after 1 'o clock. I was in the office bright and early. I was so pumped to see my team totally enthralled in the Gym Shoe Project as it become to be known as. Sandy was even there early!

Rico was at his station working away. When I saw him I immediately flashed back to last night's fantasy. I felt my cheeks burning so I went straight to my office and closed my door.

The studio was thriving. I had met with one of our Sales Reps who had come in with a new project from Manhattan Public Schools. They wanted us to design their annual report. This was a fairly easy project and I didn't want to stop the vibe so I started designing a few concepts myself.

I was occupied with the annual report and sans a few interruptions from the staff with questions; I had been in my office all day. I looked out the window at the sun setting over Manhattan and looked at the clock. It was 6 o'clock already. The hunger pangs that were rumbling through my stomach reminded me that I hadn't had lunch either. I opened my "junk drawer" and saw a Slim-fast snack bar, a package of Ramen Noodles and a Slim Jim. I wasn't happy. I made my way to the break room in hopes of finding a bag of popcorn to snack on. Instead I found Rico Matthews.

"We have to stop meeting like this," he said with a grin.

"I agree. What's new with you? I've been working on the Manhattan P.S. Annual Report all day so I didn't get a chance to come around," I said.

"Yeah, I know. I was anxiously anticipating a visit from the HWIC."

"What or who is that?" I asked.

'The Head Woman In Charge, silly" he said and pushed my shoulder lightly. Why did I feel electric currents in the space he had touched me, minutes after?

"Oh my bad! Don't be gassing me up like that. We are a team. There is no "I" in team. I'm just here to pull it all together." I replied as I searched the cabinets for some popcorn. I finally found it but of course it was on the highest shelf. As I was turning around to ask for his assistance, Rico reached over my shoulder and grabbed a bag. I was sandwiched between the counter and his body. He got the bag down and gave it to me. I waited for him to move but he didn't.

I could smell his cologne, which happened to be Dolce & Gabbana, my favorite. He was at least 8 inches taller than me which allowed me to survey his beautiful full lips. This was too much for me so I moved to the microwave.

"So Sequoia, have we sunken so low that we have to eat popcorn for dinner? Let me take you somewhere," he asked.

"Really, I'm fine Rico. I still have some work to do and I was gonna try to get that done and go on home. But thank you for offering."

'The invitation is open. Whenever you are available, I'll make sure that I am too."

"How can you eave me with an open invitation? I'm sure with all your "friends" that's purely impossible to be available at all times," I flirted back.

"I already told you, I only have friends. So no one is in the position to get upset about anything. Besides you make yourself available for the things that interest you."

"So I interest you?"

"Anyone that isn't intrigued by an intelligent, beautiful woman is a fool. My mama didn't raise no fool. Now the question is when are you gonna be available?"

I was saved by the beeping of the microwave signaling that my popcorn was done. I poured the bag into a bowl and sat down at the break room table. I was wrong for flirting and I knew it. I had to right my wrong.

"I don't think there is anything wrong with two co-workers going out to a friendly lunch or dinner. I just have to find the time. There are plenty of things for us to go over."

"Are you trying to convince me or yourself, Sequoia? I know you have a man. I'm not trying to break up a good thing but I must admit I like what I see. I work for you and I respect that, but I am a man."

He was so fine it was sickening. He had a way of looking at me that made me melt. He was sitting on the table top looking down on me and I could still smell that damn cologne! It was turning me on.

"I don't know how good my "thing" is right now. But I'm not worried about you messing it up. I just don't mix business with pleasure. It complicates things." I said as I got up to go back to my office.

"Why don't you take a look at some of the concepts I've come up with?" he asked.

I quickly agreed eager to get off of the present conversation. The production area is dimly lit due to the glare that the fluorescent lights give off on the computer screens. He had brought in a lamp for his desk and spruced the area up with pictures. It looked really nice actually. I took a seat in his "guest" chair. As we searched through the different Photoshop files that he had created, there were times when we were very close together and I found it very hard to concentrate.

I pointed out a halo that needed to be erased over one of the models he had chosen. I picked up the pen to work on it and my hand was shaking like Don Knotts. He put his hand over mine and traced over the halo. He leaned in and kissed me. I kissed him back.

I knew it was wrong but it felt so right. Here I am in a isolated place with a drop dead gorgeous man who is so much like me it is pathetic, we share the same interest, know the same people yet, I belonged to someone else.

I let him run his fingers through my layered hair and felt those familiar electric currents. He massaged my back as he kissed me and I held on for dear life. I stood between his legs as he sat on the desk and we kissed like two lovers that had been separated for months. He moved my hair and kissed my neck. His beard rubbed against my face, leaving evidence of friction, I didn't care. He placed my hand on his growing erection and I rubbed up and down the shaft through his pants. He rubbed my breast as our kiss became more passionate. I wanted more but I pulled away.

"Rico this is wrong," I said as I straightened my clothes and finger combed my hair.

"What's wrong about two people that are attracted to each other kissing?" asked Rico

"Ok I take that back. I'm wrong for doing this because I am involved with someone."

"I'm not trying to force you to do anything that you don't want to do Sequoia. But it's obvious that you want me as much as I want you."

'That may be true Rico. But we need to slow it down because I need a chance to think about things."

"What? I'm not asking you to marry me." He said.

"What the fuck does that mean? You just are trying to get a piece of ass. Well you picked the wrong chick. You caught me at a vulnerable time Rico, but I'm not a hoe," I said as I pushed past him.

"Wait a minute Sequoia," He said as he grabbed my arm and turned me around to face him. I snatched my arm away but was still mesmerized enough to stand there and see what he had to say.

"I didn't mean it like that Sequoia. What I meant was that we both have been caught off guard by this attraction and I know about your situation and I respect it. Like, I respect you. I know you aren't a hoe. I would have never been this attracted to you if I thought you were. It is just tripping me out how much I think about you and maybe I took it a little far today and I apologize."

I was tripping that he had been thinking about me too.

"I'm sorry. I didn't mean to snap at you. I guess I'm a little overwhelmed myself." I said as I felt my cheeks burning.

"I'll give you some space but that doesn't mean I want to just let this go. I mean I know you have a man but what about my feelings?" asked Rico.

"Let's just try to keep things professional for now ok? It's hard for me too. But I have to consider everything."

For a minute we stood there and finally he broke the spell by extending his hand and we walked back to his desk and continued to work on the project until I had to go.

Later on I met my Mom for dinner at her favorite Chinese Restaurant. She was really excited about my project. As always, my Mom was the most supportive person in my life. Though initially she was disappointed that I had chosen the advertising field but with all my achievements I had made her proud.

She told me how my Dad was going crazy from retirement and had even started pressuring her to retire so that they could travel the world. That was typical of my Dad. It was all about him. He was like my Mom's second child but it worked for her so who was I to complain. But I know the courts were my mother's passion. Justice was her motivation and she was relentless in the struggle. I only hoped to become half of the woman that my mother is and I'd be perfect.

Of course she inquired about Kenyon and if we had made any progress towards the altar. I immediately had flashed back to my close encounter at work. I knocked my glass of water over.

"Sequoia what is wrong with you? You've seemed distracted since you got here. Is something going on between you and Kenyon?" My Mom asked out of genuine concern.

"No mama, nothing out of the ordinary," I assured her as I wiped up my mess. I hated to lie to her but my mother had a tendency to get more involved than I liked her to. We finished up and promised to meet again next week.

Nika called on my way to the loft and I wanted to tell her about Rico so bad but I thought better of it. I think I should keep this all under my hat for right now. I hadn't heard from Kenyon all day. I assumed he was still mad, like he had a right to be. I swear niggas think they are always right. I refused to let him switch the blame on me. Even though yesterday was totally innocent, I couldn't say the same for today.

He Said…

I decided to skip work and do something I hadn't done in a while. I went to the cemetery to visit my brother's grave. I would sometimes just sit there to get a piece of mind. Today I had a lot on my mind, like planning my next move. I had fucked up royally.

When I arrived at the plot, to my surprise my sister was standing there with a bag in her hand. She had come to clean around Lavon's grave.

"Hey Janee what you doing here?"

"Just came down to clean around Von's grave. Whenever I start to miss him I come down here. I remember how much fun we used to have. I swear God blessed me with some cool brothers."

"Yeah, we did have some good times, didn't we? But you've always been a good girl so we actually are blessed to have you. That's why I got you the bomb ass going away gift."

"What do you mean going away?"

"Well Janee mom is letting you go to Spelman but you have to keep at least a B average while you are there or you are coming home."

"Oh my god Ken. I love you so much!" she said jumping up and down like she had hit the lotto. "I have to call Koi. She said if mom let me go she was going to take me shopping! So I can be ready for the men in the Atlanta. She said between the beautiful women and the gay men, I had some fierce competition!"

"See that's why mom didn't want you to go ….."

"I'm just playing calm down. Hey, you never said why you were here."

"I just came down here to clear my head and think."

"Is everything alright?"

"Yeah just work but I'm fine. Besides I missed Von so I came down here to get my mind right, that's all."

"I love you so much and that's on everything. I swear you're the best, thanks for everything."

"Just thank me by getting good grades."

"I'm gonna make you so proud."

"You already have baby girl. You already have."

Janee left and I sat there wondering why my life was going through so many changes. I mean I have it all, a great family, an awesome job and a beautiful woman. Yet, I am sitting here crying at my brother's gravesite.

So many questions were swirling around in my head. Why the hell is my life so horrible? Why did my brother have to die? Why did I eat my co-workers pussy? And why the hell did I lead Kim on?

I just wish all this madness would go away. At that moment I decided what I really needed was a vacation. On this vacation I am going to let it all go for my woman. I was going to show her that she held the key to my heart and soul. And the ring that I was going to give her was going to be a symbol that proved it.

I made a few calls and headed to the office. I was sitting in my office waiting for the jeweler to come with the 5 rings I had picked out a few months ago. I was finally going to pick out "The One".

Buzz, buzz.

"Yes."

"Kenyon, there are two gentlemen here from the NYPD here to see you and they want to see you now."

"Fuck!" I thought to myself. "What the hell do they want? Send them in thanks. Shanice, when the jeweler comes tell him that I'll be with him in a few."

"Not a problem," she said with an attitude.

I couldn't help but think about her independence speech from last night. "I won't get in your way." What had happened to that? I wondered as I watched two police officers enter my office.

"Hello Mr. Burnett. I am Detective Shaw and this is my partner Detective Williams. We're here to place you under arrest for the domestic attack on Kimberly Bell. You have the right to…."

"What the hell is going on?" I asked as Detective Shaw grabbed me roughly by the arm.

"Mr. Burnett you are making this harder than it has to be."

"Look Mr. Shaw, I really don't know what the hell is going on."

"Mr. Burnett this will be straightened out when we get to the station."

"Well can we please just walk out of here without any hand cuffs? I'm not trying to get away. I'm a professional not a criminal."

"You should have thought about that before you decided to choke the hell out of Ms. Bell. Now let's go."

As they were taking me out, all of my co-workers were looking and whispering. How the hell am I going to explain this shit to Koi and my parents?

As we walked down the hall I yelled to Shanice, "Call my lawyer. His number is in my phone book, Richard Walls. Tell him to get to the police station now!"

Shanice responded with a sneaky smirk on her face. All I knew is that bitch better make that call or there would be hell to pay.

He Said…She Said

Chapter 7

She Said…

*S*o Nika and I decided to hang out. I still had not heard from Kenyon and he wasn't at the loft when I got there to change my clothes. I showered and changed into a pair of jeans and a tank top. I dressed the outfit up with my big hoop earrings, a bad-ass belt and a pair of Jimmy Choo heels. I pulled my hair off my face and threw on a leather jacket and left. I thought about leaving a note but figured "what the hell?"

I called Nika when I was outside of her apartment. She, as usual, was looking fabulous. She had on a pair of Seven jeans with a over-sized scarf tied around her waist, over her breast and around her neck.

"What's up hoochie?" I asked her when she got in the car.

"Nothing girl. I wanna be like you when I grow up Ma," she said eyeing my car. She was rubbing the leather like she wasn't used to it.

"Yeah right, I wanna be like your ass." I said laughing.

"So what prompted your ass to come out tonight? You know you usually don't have time for your girl," said Nika, as she put on some lip gloss.

"Girl, I'm busy as hell, but I needed a break today. You know get out, have some drinks, mix and mingle."

"So you're having problems with that no-good ass nigga of yours," said Nika matter-of-factly.

"Just because I want to go out doesn't mean that we're having problems," I said defending my relationship.

"Tell that to someone that doesn't know girl. We've been friends for damn near forever and I know you and I know that Negro too. I told you that you should've done a little more than you did to his ass. He didn't learn his lesson. You're too easy on his ass." She said rolling her eyes.

"Nika chill out. I said there's nothing going on. We're fine. I just wanted to get out, that's all," I explained and slapped myself mentally for it because that just showed that she was right.

"Um-hmm, whatever you say baby. Just know that your girl gotcha back and if we have to roll down on his ass, we will."

We were both silent for a while as I drove down 122nd Street. Both in our own little worlds.

Nika

She ain't slick. I know that nigga has her upset again. I knew before when his ass was messing around and I know he is now. But you can't tell Sequoia shit about her man. I know that's the first piece of real dick that she's had but damn, he got her ass sprung! I told her before that I could introduce her to bigger and better things. This nigga ain't worth all the grief that he has put her through. He know I got my ear to the street and when I find out this time, there ain't no holding back because she deserves better. She's smart as hell, successful and drop dead gorgeous. She can have any man she wants...I just hope he doesn't hurt her again.

She Said…

When we got to the club it was jumping. We used the valet service as usual and Nika walked to the front of the line like she was somebody and obviously she was because we were whisked in by the bouncer.

We sat down at the bar and were immediately approached by two lame ass men. "What you ladies drinking tonight?" asked one of the lames.

"We'll have a bottle of Cristal, thank you," said Nika as she straightened her scarf, I mean shirt.

"That's a bit expensive for my blood," said the lame.

"That's what we're drinking. So I guess we'll see you later," said Nika as I held my laugh in the best I could.

When he walked away I bust out laughing. I always said Nika was cruel for using that one on guys. Her motto was "why waste twenty minutes of club time on a lame? He was just blocking action from the guy that you really wanted to get to know."

After Nika had secured us a bottle of Cristal, compliments of an "old flame," we ventured over to the "Lounge."

The Lounge is where all the VIP's were sitting. Once you were granted access to the Lounge, you were liable to see movie stars, athletes, rappers, anybody that was somebody. And of course Nika had no problem getting in.

Fortunately I wasn't star-struck because I'd worked with so many celebrities in my business that it wasn't anything to me. Besides in New York, "celebrity sightings" are the norm. I immediately saw the members of Cash the Check Records, a record label that we had done a marketing and advertising plan for. I went over and spoke to them and felt Nika burning a hole in my back with her stare.

"Hey guys let me introduce you to my best friend Nika," I said as she did her thing, flirting with them all.

"Sequoia, we need to get together soon. We are doing another promotional contest and I want to see what you can come up with," said James, one of the twins.

"Not a problem Jay. You know I got you. Call me tomorrow and we'll get right on it."

I had to literally drag Nika away from them. She was such a hound it was pathetic. "Don't tell me. Let me guess. Now you want to be in one of their videos," I asked her.

"Stop hating Sequoia. I would never be a video hoe. But I wouldn't mind getting to know that one guy better. So I might just happen to walk in on your meeting tomorrow," she said as she glanced back at the guys.

"First off tomorrow is only a phone call not a meeting and you will not come on my job soliciting for a man," I laughed.

"Girl, you know I love the bling-bling and those boys were bling-blinging baby."

We found an open space to chill and survey the crowd. We were approached by several different men. I was enjoying myself and had completely forgotten about Kenyon and our problems. I excused myself to go to the restroom. Much to my surprise there wasn't a line. It was just me and two other girls that seemed to be together.

I unbuckled my jeans and did my business and listened to their conversation.

Girl#1 – Girl, it is popping in here! I didn't think it was going to be this crowded. I hope I don't bump into old boy. That's all I need.

Girl # 2 – I heard that. Is he still calling you?

Girl # 1 – Periodically. I guess whenever he gets bored with his woman.

Girl # 2 – Bianca, pass me a piece of paper towel.

My heart practically dropped into my stomach. Did I just hear the name Bianca? Suddenly I was seeing red. I burst out the stall but they had already left out. I must have drunk too much Cristal because I couldn't even remember how they looked.

I splashed some water on my face and slowly began to rationalize the situation. "Ok Sequoia, there is more than one Bianca in this world. And that one doesn't have to be the one I'm looking for. Besides I believe that bitch lives in Chicago, so why would she be here in the middle of the week?" I regrouped and went back out to join Nika. I couldn't let that shit bug me. I poured myself another flute of champagne and tried to relax.

My favorite R. Kelly song came on and I was dancing in place. I felt someone tap me on the shoulder. I was so mad

56

thinking to myself "Damn I can't even dance by myself without someone running up and asking me to dance." I turned around with a scowl on my face, only to see Rico staring at me.

"What are you doing here?" I asked still reeling in shock.

"No, what are you doing here? I thought you were going to dinner with your Mom and then going home," said Rico.

"Well after everything that's happened, I decided I needed a drink or two or three," I said jokingly, waving my flute in front of me.

"I definitely understand. But a cold shower is what I really needed. I only came here to meet my brother and his friends for a quick drink and I'm out."

I don't know where it came from but I heard myself asking him could I go home with him.

"Are you sure Koi? A few hours ago you needed time to think about everything."

"I just don't want to go home Rico. We don't have to do anything." I said sounding really desperate.

"That's fine with me. Let's go." He said taking my hand.

"I have to go tell my girl where I am going." I went to look for Nika and didn't have to look far. She was schmoozing with my record label friends. I told her I was leaving and she could take my car home. She said she was actually riding home with her new friend so she didn't need the car. I gave her the mean look and made her promise to call me when she made it home on my cell.

As I am following Rico to his apartment, I'm suddenly overwhelmed with guilt. What am I doing? I asked myself. I didn't want to bail again because I didn't want him to think I was some psycho bitch but I wasn't sure if I wanted to go to his apartment anymore. When we pulled into his parking garage and found a spot, I realized my hands were sore because I had been gripping the steering wheel so tight during my anxiety attack. I took a deep breath and opened my door. Rico was waiting.

Kim

I showed that stupid mutha fucka. I told him I wasn't going to let his ass go. I mean what the fuck does his bitch have on me anyway? I look good as hell and I make good money. I guess that's not enough for a man like Ken. He wants some high profile bitch. Well let's see how his bitch handles this shit. I swear I am going to ruin his relationship with this bitch if it's the last thing I do.

Kim's thought was interrupted by the shrill sound of the ringing telephone.

"Hello, Ms. Bell this is Det. Shaw. I just wanted to inform you that we have Mr. Burnett in our custody. We need you to come down and make a statement before he goes in front of the judge to be arraigned."

"Well I can't come right now."

"Well if you don't come and press charges and give your statement we will have to let him go."

"Just tell that son of a bitch to stay the hell away from me."

"Don't tell me that you are not going to press charges against him."

"This time I'll let him off. Just tell him to stay away from me."

"You seemed so adamant about him being caught for what he'd done to you. Are you really sure this is what you want?"

"That's what I said."

"I can't believe you aren't going to press charges."

"I don't give a damn what you believe now leave me alone."

I think the shock of the police coming to get his ass was enough and when he finds out I didn't press charges maybe he will know how much I truly love his ass. Maybe he will realize that if I can't have him no one will."

"Mr. Burnett today is your lucky day. Ms. Bell has decided not to press charges on your sorry ass."

I breathed a sigh of relief and responded, "Oh really? She's finally come to her senses. I told you I was innocent, yet you still chose to treat me like some ghetto ass nigga anyway. You get no respect since you took me out of my office in damn handcuffs. But if I was some rich white boy you would have never treated me like that, would you Detective Shaw?

"Race has nothing to do with it Mr. Burnett. You were accused of a violent crime. I followed the proper procedures to detain you. Besides, you know how you brothas can get," said Det. Shaw with emphasis on the word brothas.

"Proper procedures my ass. This was just another feeble attempt on your part to try to make a successful black man look bad. You hate it that I'm young, black and rich don't you? I'm not like you Detective Shaw, living paycheck to paycheck. Worrying about how I'm going to pay my rent. I'm a success story, not a ghetto ass nigga. Just because some stupid ass girl decides too cry wolf you automatically assume it's another nigga beating on his woman. I might be a sorry mutha fucka but if I'm sorry and I have all this I wonder what the fuck you are?"

"You son of ..."

"Excuse me. My name is Mr. Walls. I'm Mr. Burnett's attorney. I think you are totally out of line and this won't go over well with your boss."

"Don't worry about it Richard. He's just upset because he's just been upstaged by a black man."

"Well Ken, I assume we're done conducting business here. Let's get you out of here."

"Yeah, let's go. Oh, by the way Detective Shaw, this is what a $2000 an hour lawyer will get you. See you later brotha."

As we got into his car, Mr. Walls filled me in on what had happened with Kim.

"So she dropped the charges?"

"She never pressed them and you're lucky she didn't. I hope you've learned your lesson."

"Most definitely. Thanks for everything. Send the bill to my office please. I'll see you soon."

"Don't make it too soon Kenyon," said Mr. Walls as he pulled up in front of the apartment.

I got home a little after 3 am and my woman wasn't at home. At first, I was mad but at the same time I wouldn't have to explain my day to her and that was certainly a relief. I checked my voicemail and much to my surprise, there was no message from Koi.

I took a shower to freshen up and get my mind together. I thought about how I was going to handle going back to the office and where my woman could possibly be at 3 o'clock in the morning. I decided to just wait until she came in instead of calling. I called myself resting my eyes but when I opened them up again it was 6:48 and Sequoia Johnson was no where to be found.

She Said…

I cannot believe I'm doing this. I walked down the stairs behind him to his apartment. My hands are shaking like Don Knotts! I check out that apartment and am reassured that it's definitely a bachelor's pad. The décor was done in blacks and grays. He told me to relax and went to hang our coats.

"Relax? Yeah right!" I thought to myself. I start rubbing my hands together to stop them from shaking. "This is what you asked for Koi. Stop tripping!"

Rico walked back into living room and I almost fainted. He had taken his shirt off. He was ripped to say the least. He offered me a drink. I gladly accepted.

"Come on in here and help me," said Rico as he pulled me up from the couch.

"I'm a guest. You should be serving me." I softly replied.

I surveyed his liquor collection and decided on margaritas. I salted the rims of the glasses and added ice. He poured the tequila and I added the mix. He topped them off with 3 olives per drink. When he handed me my drink, he noticed my hand was shaking. I cursed myself silently.

"What's with the shaking? Do I make you nervous?" he asked as he set the drinks down and grabbed me by my waist and pulled me closer to him.

"No, it's not you. It's just that…I don't do stuff like this." I stammered along trying to explain myself.

"We haven't done anything, Koi," Rico replied jokingly.

"I know. I'm just afraid that we might."

"I promise I won't make you do anything that you don't want to do." He said as he ran his fingers through my hair and massaged my scalp. I started to loosen up as he kneaded my shoulders. I lifted my head to receive the gentle kisses that he had for me.

My hands explored his bare chest and I noticed they were no longer shaking. I wanted this more than ever. I wanted to feel him inside of me. I became more eager with each kiss. I desperately tried to hold on to my sanity as I kissed him with more passion than I'd felt for anyone in a long time.

We moved from the kitchen to his bedroom. I let him undress me until I lay on the bed in my Victoria Secret thong and nothing else. I watched as he completely undressed in front of me. My eyes explored every inch of his body. I was hungry for him. I sat up and kissed his stomach and traced, with my tongue the trail of fine hair that started at his naval and ended at his pubic hair. I kissed his penis and took him into my mouth. I tasted his sweetness. I became more eager to have it all in my mouth. I rapidly sucked, kissed, licked and stroked him until he couldn't take it anymore. He pushed me back onto the bed and ripped my thong off. He turned me over on my stomach and forced his way in. I gasped and pushed back on his penis, making him thrust even harder. This was no longer making love. We were fucking and I liked it. I thought about Kenyon once and that bitch Bianca. I wondered is this what they did behind my back. Was this how she was feeling as my man fucked the shit out of her? I momentarily felt sick but I regained my composure as I let this man run my body. I gave myself to him and used every inch of my being to satisfy him. I hate Kenyon for the things he had put me through. I hated Rico for coming into my life and making me realize that I was not satisfied with my life. I hate myself for being so weak that I didn't want to change it.

As we lay together in puddle of sweat I listen to him snore softly. I rearrange my head on his shoulder and fix my earring so that it won't poke me in the neck. My hair is soaked and a few stray strands stick to the side of my face. I smell the undeniable scent of lust. There had been no love in this room. Pure lust. There was something behind the De'Rico Matthews story too. I have problems but he was releasing some frustration as well. I played with his hair and fell asleep.

Chapter 8

9 woke up three hours later. I showered and put my clothes back on. I told Rico I would be in the office a little later and I would see him there.

As soon as I got into the car, I called Nika. She answered the phone extra groggy and obviously hung over.

"Hello" she croaked.

"Hey, it's me. Has Kenyon called there?"

"No. Where the hell are you?"

"I'm on my way home, but I wanted to make sure he hadn't called there because you are my alibi."

'You little wench! You stayed out all night. What the hell got into you?" said Nika sitting up in her bed.

"I don't know Nika. I'm just tired I guess. I don't what has gotten into me. Just have my back if he calls. I'll call you when I get to work."

"You better make sure you have your story straight."

"I do. I'll call you later."

"Ok. Ciao."

I hung up and gave a sigh of relief. He hadn't called. Now that was a surprise. Actually that was not like Kenyon at all. He had a tendency to be a little overbearing at times.

I walked in the door at 7 o'clock prepared to receive the Riot Act but he was fast asleep. At least I thought he was.

"Where were you last night?" he asked still lying down.

"Out. Why?" I replied.

"Just out? Why didn't you come home Sequoia?"

"Who are you Ken? My man or my father? We got a bit too tipsy last night so I stayed over Nika's. Is that alright?"

"Over Nika's, huh? Since when did you start getting so drunk on a weeknight knowing that you have to go to work the next day?" he asked sitting up in the bed.

"First of all, I'm a grown ass woman. And if I decide that I would rather not risk my life trying to drive home drunk just so that I don't upset you, is my business." I said as I went into the bathroom to undress for my shower. He was hot on my tail.

"So it's like that now, huh? You stay out all night and don't think to call? That's how we're doing things now?" he asked.

I felt a small snap in my brain and I literally saw a flash of light. "What the fuck do you mean it's like that now? It's been like that for you Kenyon! How many fucking nights have I been here waiting for you to come home and you never make it or call? So what the fuck is so different about my situation Kenyon? What's different about today? Oh I see, you're just afraid that I might have been out doing the same thing that you were doing right? Well guess what nigga? You'll never know!"

We stood there for a few seconds staring at each other and he looked like he was ready to tear my head off but I was so mad I was ready for anything he threw in my direction.

"Fine Koi. If you want to be a hoe, then do your thing."

"Did you just call me a hoe?"

"If the shoe fits."

"You're pathetic. I've taken too much shit off of you Kenyon but you will not disrespect me to my face."

I grabbed my robe and walked out of the bathroom. I threw on some sweats and gym shoes and grabbed my purse and slammed the door on my way out.

He Said…

"Man, I can't believe she walked her ass in this house and caught an attitude with me. I was here all night. Well once I got out of jail but she don't know nothing about that. I know damn well she wasn't over that bitch Nika's house because Koi is funny about staying anywhere. And I know damn well she

64

wasn't that drunk because she don't ever get that fucked up. Koi is way too responsible to do something so stupid." I realized that I was still standing in the bathroom, alone, so I went back into our bedroom. The bedroom that I'd slept in last night by my damn self.

"I really think she stayed out to prove a point and to be honest I wish she really hadn't done that. I'm doing everything in my power to make this thing we call a relationship work but I can't do it alone. Ever since I saw her with that guy I've noticed a change in her entire attitude and it's truly not for the best. She's become disrespectful and I ain't having that. She's always had a smart mouth but she has always kept it respectful. I don't know what has come over her but I know this is not the same ole' Koi. All I have to say is my woman better come back because this shit ain't cool."

I began to get ready for work and please believe I really wasn't ready to face all my coworkers and I damn sure wasn't ready to answer any questions about yesterday. I have to admit, I was really embarrassed. For something like that to happen to me not only makes me look bad but my parents and Koi's father. "I really am feeling bad but hey, it couldn't be avoided."

The way my morning was going I knew the first person to say the wrong thing to me was going to feel the wrath that was really meant for Koi. So I got myself mentally prepared for the worse. When I got off the elevator I noticed that it suddenly got really quiet and everybody started whispering as soon as I walked by. I could only imagine what they were saying. So I made my way to my office and Shanice gave a message I really didn't want to hear. Mr. Johnson wanted me to call him as soon as I got to the office. "Damn," I thought to myself. "Does he know what happened? Did he call the precinct and found out I was down there because I had choked the shit out of the lady that I just happen to have been cheating on his daughter with?"

I went in my office and checked my voicemails. There was a message from my mom and also Mr. Johnson. I really didn't want to speak to neither of them right now but I knew I had to call Mr. Johnson back and since I didn't know what was going on with Koi, he might know what the hell was her deal.

I buzzed Shanice.

"Yes Mr. Burnett, can I help you?"

I couldn't believe this simple ass hoe had the nerve to have on her professional face today.

"Yes can you get Mr. Johnson on the phone for me?"

"No problem. Is there anything else I can do for you?"

I could hear the smirk in her voice. "No that's it."

After about five minutes my line rung.

"Sederick how's everything?" I asked hoping for the best.

"Not too good Kenyon. I've heard some disturbing things about you. I think we need to meet for lunch so we can discuss exactly what would have the police at my office, dragging my future son-in-law out like some common criminal."

"There's a good explanation for this Sederick. I'll meet you. Give me the time and place."

"How about 1 o'clock at the Choices Soul food on 105th?"

"That's fine. I'll see you then."

I knew from that point on I was in for a very difficult day. I packed up a few files and decided it'd be easier to work from home. I stopped by the florist to grab Koi a dozen roses to take to her office. I was going to tell her that no matter what I still loved her and I'm sorry about this morning. I also decided I was going to tell her about what happened the night I left.

When I opened the door to the lobby I was greeted by their snobbish receptionist.

"May I help you?"

"Now this lady has seen me a million times. She knows who I am here for. Why is she messing with me?" I thought to myself. But I figured I'd be the bigger person. "Good morning. I'm here to see Sequoia Johnson, is she available?"

"I'm sorry but Ms. Johnson isn't in today. Would you like to leave her a message?"

"Naw, I'm straight," I said as I threw the flowers in the waste basket and left like I'd just lost the only woman I've truly loved.

"Where the hell could she be?" I couldn't worry too much about that though because I had to get my story straight for my lunch meeting with Mr. Johnson.

"Damn, what else can go wrong?"

He Said…She Said

Chapter 9

She Said…

I couldn't believe he was reacting the way he was. How dare he question me about anything? Even though I knew I was dead wrong! He was still the pot calling the kettle black.

I suddenly realized that I was driving aimlessly. I pulled over to gather my senses. The first thing I realized is that I had on a Roc-A-Wear jogging suit and I couldn't wear that to work. Second thing I realized is I hadn't showered. Right then I decided I needed a "personal day." Lord knows I deserved one. I hardly ever miss work and if I do, I'm working from home.

I pulled off and headed to the mall. I went to Victoria's Secrets and purchased two beautiful bra and panty sets. Tyra don't have a thing on me! I also grabbed a pair of comfy pajamas and a robe. I went into Macy's and bought a killer Donna Karan suit and a pair of Ferragamo shoes for tomorrow. I ventured into the Juniors' area and copped a pair of jeans and a sweater.

I checked into the Waldorf Astoria Hotel in a master suite complete with a fireplace and personal chef. I grabbed a few snacks and two mystery novels from the gift shop and went to my suite showered and got in the bed.

Finally I was able to relax. My body felt as if I'd been punished. I guess Rico had put a whupping on my ass. I was still shuddering from the multiple orgasms I'd had. My mind drifted back to last night as he rocked inside of me, begging me to cum with him.

I felt that familiar tingle in my center. "I've got to stop thinking about him."

I called Nika to let her know where I was but told her I would be turning my cell phone off so to call the room directly if she needed me.

"Gone with your bad ass. I'm proud of you Koi. I can't believe you've finally wised up and stepped out…"

I cut her off mid-sentence.

"Nika, I'm not trying to hear this right now. I just need to rest."

"Old Rico-Suave must have worn your ass out," laughed Nika.

"Bye-girl!" I said as I hung up before she could say anything else.

I called the office to check my voicemail and let Mr. Reed know that I would be checking my voicemail and email throughout the day and would put out any fires tomorrow.

"There I'm done. No interruptions or distractions. Only relaxation."

The suite phone rang. "What the hell does she want?"

"What Nika!!" I yelled into the phone.

"Uh, this isn't Nika. It's Rico."

"Oh I um… thought you were…um… How did you know I was here?" I asked.

"I saw you walk in the door. And judging from the look on your face, I figured you looked too disturbed to be meeting your man. So I called the front desk," he said so casually like it was ok that he'd called my room. "So was I wrong?" he asked.

"No, actually you hit the nail right on the head. I just needed some time to myself. So I'm gonna get off this phone and chill out. I'll talk to you later," I said because I couldn't think of anything else to say to this man that had turned my world upside down in a matter of days.

"Well, I'll let you go but if you need to talk, you know the number," said Rico.

"Thanks. Well ok, I'll see you tomorrow."

I hung up the phone but I could smell his cologne like he was lying right next to me. I smelled the shower fresh scent of his shampoo like his dreads were hanging in my face.

"Damn, I'm bugging. What the hell am I going to do with myself? My man basically called me a hoe today and this man is treating me like a queen. I need to pump my brakes and take some time to think all of this through."

As I pulled the covers up to my chin, I wondered what Kenyon was doing.

He Said…

One o'clock came a lot faster than I thought it would. And with that time came the uneasiness of meeting Koi's dad. When I arrived he was dressed in his normal gear, beige Ralph Lauren khakis and black polo styled shirt. He'd just come from his morning golf game and judging by the way he was joking with someone on his cell phone he done pretty well. As he saw me approaching the table he closed his conversation and greeted me a hand shake and hug, done all at once like he'd seen the young guys do on television. I knew then he wasn't as mad as I'd thought he would be.

"Ken! How's my future son-in-law?"

"I'm good. A little stressed with work and personal things going on with the family, but I know you didn't call me here to ask me that. I know you want me to tell you about yesterday."

"Of course I do and besides that we haven't had our usual Sunday morning golf game. What? You scared of an old man whooping your butt?" He said laughing so hard he had to take a drink of water to stop from choking.

"I don't know about the scared part but yes I am tired of losing to you, but its cool I've been practicing. I'll be ready for you in a couple weeks."

"Good, so tell me about yesterday. Ken is it anything I can do?"

"Well what happened is a long story and to be honest a huge misunderstanding. I was taken down to the station on ludicrous charge for something I didn't do."

"What was the charge?"

"My ex said I assaulted her. Choked her to be exact." Right away I saw the expression on his face completely change. He seemed to be saying "What the fuck is my daughter about to marry?"

"Before you ask I didn't choke her or anybody else all the charges were dropped within a hour of them taking me to jail."

"Dropped? Why would she do something so ridiculous? What's gotten into her?" Mr. Johnson asked as he sipped his water.

"Sir I really don't know. I haven't messed around with her since I've been with Sequoia." I said as convincingly as I could. It didn't work.

"Come on Ken. I'm a man too. I know that you've cheated on my daughter. Shit I've cheated on her mother but the thing is you don't get caught! You're a smart guy Ken. Come on son, you have a great lady in my daughter. You really don't want to mess that up do you?"

I have to admit I was taken by total surprise with his straightforwardness about being a man and knowing the things men go through.

"Ok, I used to mess around with her but I haven't in a long time. I just wish she would leave me alone." I noticed that we'd been talking for a while and no waitress had come to our table yet. "Man the service here is terrible. No one has come to ask if we even wanted some water."

"Actually the service is great. I asked them to let us talk for a minute and I ordered for us already." Just as he was saying that our food was coming. He'd ordered us both catfish with greens made with turkey, macaroni and cheese, and cornbread. As the waitress sat the food down she asked, "Did you gentlemen want something to drink?"

"Yes, do you have Voss?" I asked.

"We sure do."

"I'll have that." Mr. Johnson just got normal water and we finished our conversation as we ate.

"Mr. Johnson, I can be frank with you. I have done my dirt but I know that Koi is the woman for me. No one in my past compares to her and I want to marry her as soon as I can. But something has been different about her lately." I decided to keep this new coworker under my cap for a minute.

"Well you know she has this gym shoe project at work now. Maybe she is stressed about work. Just give it a minute, things will be back to normal soon. You know how she is about her work. She got it honest. Which brings me back to yesterday. Whatever you have going on Ken, get it under control. One thing you will learn is that what ever dirt you do in the streets; you leave it in the streets. Nothing should ever touch the home front and that includes your business. I trust and respect you. Keep it that way," he said as he pulled out his credit card to pay.

"Please, I'll take care of it. I appreciate you talking to me Mr. Johnson. You have my word that nothing will ever reach the home front again," I said as I signed the bill.

"Ken, thanks for lunch. Get your stuff together and if you need me give me a call."

"I sure will. Thanks again."

We left the restaurant and went our separate ways and my problems seemed minimal; at least the one at work but the one at home was still there. I was looking but I didn't see it coming to an end anytime soon.

I got home and Koi still wasn't there and it was really starting to bother me. I knew that it was going to get a lot worse before it got better. So I turned my Lyfe CD on and started looking over all my files, diving head first into the Roberts file. I was working away when the door man buzzed me and said I had a package. I asked him to send it up. When I opened the package it was a package from my mom with a note that read:

Ken,
I was out and saw this mp3 player and thought it was
so cute! I know how much you love your music and
since you've been working out now you can do both.
The guy said it holds like three hours worth of music
so enjoy it and I will talk to you soon. Call your father
he misses you just like I do.

Love you,
Mom

P.S.
Call Janee she needs her big brother and kiss my
daughter-in-law for me.

I read the note and was about to call her when my cell phone rang. The name on the phone put a smile on my face and also a knot in my stomach. It was my *Wifey* calling.

She Said…

I was so mad about this morning but I was also feeling terribly guilty. I wanted to at least apologize for my part in the argument, so I called Ken. He answered on the second ring.

"Hello? Koi?" he said

I opened my mouth but the words wouldn't come out. I sat there looking incredibly stupid as I listened to him calling my name.

Finally I hung up the phone. I guess I'm just not ready to face him right now. I have never, ever cheated on Ken and I feel terrible but in a way I feel vindicated. That was the scary part about it. I didn't want this to be ok. This isn't how I was raised. My mother and father had a beautiful marriage. I barely ever heard them argue. Now here I am cheating on my man. What the hell was wrong with me? I needed to sleep, to think about everything before I called him back. I turned my phone off and got back under the covers. Before I knew it I was drifting into a dream.

I had just arrived home after another night working past 8 o'clock. I already knew Kenyon was going to be tripping. I padded across the loft in my stocking feet. "He must be working out," I thought to myself as I heard the Alicia Keys Uncut CD playing. As I walked towards my bedroom I unbuttoned my blouse and let it fall off my shoulders to the floor. I was dead tired and figured I would pick it up in the morning.

As I approached the bedroom I began to hear noises that can never be mistaken. My heart began to thud in my chest as I crept to the door. "Please Lord. Don't let this be happening. Not in my own bed." I slowly pushed the door open. I saw a pair of legs wrapped around my man's back as his ass pumped up and down. Whoever it was he was fucking was thoroughly enjoying my man's skills. He kept asking her, "Whose pussy is this?" She answered between gasps and moans, "Yours Kenyon."

I stood there praying that my legs would work. Praying that I would gather my senses and turn to run away. Instead I calmly walked across the room to my dresser which held a marble statue that we bought when we went to the Bahamas the year before. I grabbed the statue and walked to the bed. The couple was too engrossed in the terrible act they were committing to even notice me.

Just then Kenyon pulled out and turned the woman over to hit it doggy-style. It was then that her identity was revealed and then that she saw me standing there.

We both screamed as I lunged towards Kenyon and my very best friend Nika!

I woke up screaming. I frantically looked around the darkened room. I had no idea where I was until my eyes adjusted to the darkness and I realized I was in my hotel suite. My face was drenched with tears and I had sweated my hair out. My pajamas were soaked and clung to my skin. My mouth was dry from screaming and crying, I assumed. I got up and padded to the mini-bar. I started for the bottled water but instead downed the miniature bottle of Johnny Walker Red.

"What the fuck was that about?"

He Said…

"Koi! Koi! Baby I know you hear me. Say something. Damn." I thought to myself she hung up. I've been trying to call her ass all day but her damn cell has been turned off and her assistant at work acts like she doesn't have clue when she's going to be back to work. This day has really been a roller coaster. I wished this joy ride would hurry up and come to an end. I sat and listened to a few songs on my new mp3 player and worked on Ms. Roberts file. Before I knew it I'd been three hours and I'd found all kinds of ways to make her a boatload of money. I still couldn't get my mind off Koi so I decided to call Colin. I wanted to go have a drink at Tonic, this little jazz bar Koi and I go to.

We arrived at the bar about 9 pm. I told Colin that there would be no talk about the ladies in our lives. This was going to be a boy's night out.

"Damn Ken I really needed this man. Ever since I found out..."

"Man I told you no talking about women. Damn, order yourself a drink."

"Order me a Heineken while I go drain the snake."

"Okay bet."

We were sitting at the bar and there is a huge mirrored wall that allows you to see the entire bar behind you. As I checked out the ladies in the club, I couldn't help but to think about Koi. Then I noticed someone who looked really familiar. I turned around to get a better view. Yep, I was right. It was the guy she was with at Justin's. I just sat there and got even more pissed. When the bartender came and asked me what I wanted, I was still staring at this guy that had my woman so into him that she didn't answer my call.

"Sir, can I get you something? SIR! can I get you something?" he asked again.

"I'm sorry my mind is somewhere else. You can get me two Heinekens and give me two shots of Remy XO."

"Will that be all?" he asked seeming a little irritated.

"Yes for now. Can I run a tab?"

"Yes but I'll need a credit card."

I opened my wallet and pulled out my American Express Black card. "Will this one do?"

He snatched the card and walked away. What was his problem?

I saw Colin come out of the restroom but instead of coming back to the bar he stopped at the table where the guy with the dreads was sitting! "What the fuck?" I thought to myself. "How does C know that guy? Better yet, how good does he know him?" This could be my way of finding out how good Dread really knows Koi. While I was thinking of my plot to get that dread to tell me about his relationship with Koi, Colin waved me over to the table the dread and his friend were occupying. I made my way over to the table through the crowd.

"Ken, this my boy De'Rico Mathews and his boy John. Sorry John I don't remember your last name."

"Banks. John Banks."

"Thanks John. And this is my frat brother." And before he could my name out of his mouth I answered, "Keith. Keith Edwards."

Colin gave me the "What the hell is going on?" look. I would fill him in later but right now I didn't need Dread to know who I was. At least until I found out who this De'Rico was to Koi.

"Nice to meet you man," said De'Rico. I made sure he felt that extra tight grip when we shook hands.

"Same here," I responded.

"So what brings you guys out Keith? I've been trying to get Colin out ever since he and my cousin Chanelle started dating."

"Oh shit," I thought to myself. "This nigga is related to Chanelle."

"Well he works hard and believe it or not I only got him out because I was having problems of my own, and I needed his advice." Colin really started looking at me like, "What the fuck are you talking bout?"

"Really Colin? I didn't know you were the bar therapist." Dread said.

"I didn't either. Normally Ken. I mean Keith is the one with the sound advice."

"Damn this nigga better not fuck this up for me." I said to myself as I tried my hardest to send telepathic messages to Colin.

"Come on C, you know you got the best advice in the world."

"Well Colin, your boy Rico is having mad women problems." John said out of nowhere. Rico gave him the same look Colin had been giving me.

I threw my two cents in hoping he would take the bait. "Well since we're having a therapeutic session anyway, why don't you tell Colin the problem and I'm sure he'll be able to help you."

Rico hesitated a little but finally opened the conversation with, "Okay Dr. Colin here it goes. I just started this new job and I'm really attracted to my boss but the problem is she has a man and I don't think I stand a chance with her."

I'm standing there ready to pounce over the table thinking to myself, "Yea nigga, you don't stand a chance because you'll be lucky if you even make it out of this damn bar."

"So what makes you think you don't have a chance?" Colin asked.

"Well for one, she just doesn't seem like that kind of lady. She's a throw back, the kind of woman that will stick by her man not caring about all the bullshit he puts her through. But when she goes she's gone."

I'm standing here steaming. "I mean this negro really thinks he knows my woman, if in fact he's talking about my woman."

"Rico I think you should go for it; man, you only live once," said Colin as I gave him the look of death.

"Man, Colin you know that's some bullshit. Look Rico, I don't know you but I think you should leave her alone if she has a man. But if she pursues you then maybe you should go for it." I suggested.

"You know that actually makes sense Keith. Even though it might be too late to let it go. I'm really feeling her." Said Rico.

"What you think John?" Colin asked.

"I think you should say fuck her man and bang her ass and let her man worry about why his bitch is cheating."

"Yeah I'm going to jail tonight for sure," I thought to myself.

"I think I'm going to just chill. If she wants me she'll have to let me know. I gave her all I have to offer and if she liked it she'll holla at me for sure," he replied.

Now what the fuck does he means he gave her all he had to offer? I couldn't hold it in any longer. "You already fucked her?" I asked, praying he said no.

"Naw man I didn't say that. I just said I gave her the best that I had to offer. We'll see where she takes it from here."

"I feel that. Well it's been real but I gotta get out of here. Colin, you bout ready?" I asked.

"Yea man, I'm ready. Let's go. Rico and John it's been real." Colin said as he slapped hands with both men.

Rico stood up and shook my hand. "Nice meeting you Keith and thanks for the advice."

"No problem man, don't be breaking up no happy homes." I said jokingly but was serious as hell. "And nice meeting you too John."

"Same here man, same here."

As we were walking to my truck Colin asked, "What was up with all that Keith shit?"

"Man I can't really tell you everything, but I'm almost sure he was talking about Koi."

"Koi, as in Sequoia?" he said puzzled.

"Yeah my Koi. What other Koi do we know?

"Hell naw! What are you gonna do?" Colin asked looking really flabbergasted by the news.

"Man I don't know but I better hurry up and get to the bottom of this before it gets out of hand."

I dropped Colin off and looked at my watch. It read 12:15am so started to head home. As I was driving I felt an indescribable pain in my heart. I'd never felt this pain before but I'm sure Koi and many other women in my past had felt this pang before. I think my heart was broken.

I began to cry uncontrollably. I don't know if I was overwhelmed with this situation with Koi or sad about Lavon or if I was just missing Janee. I figured it was a combination of all of them. I had to think of a game plan to get back in Koi's good graces. I decided a little family trip would help us a lot. She and I should go to see Janee and while we're there we can work on us.

I rushed home to tell Koi my plan. But I was met by an empty loft. Koi was nowhere to be found.

Chapter 10

She Said…

I woke up with a killer headache. I glanced over at the clock on the nightstand. It was 1 o'clock in the morning. I was finally able to fall back to sleep after I'd downed half the damn mini-bar. Talk about cotton mouth, whew! I trudged over and opened up the eight dollar bottle of bottled water. They kill me with the prices on this shit that should be complimentary, seeing how much I was paying to stay up in this joint.

My suite had a window that stretched clear across the entire far wall of the suite affording me a magnificent view of the city that never sleeps. I was so far up I couldn't see the hustle and bustle that I was sure was still going on in the streets but the city lights were so calming.

How did I get in this mess? I asked myself. I love Kenyon but when do you say when? There has always been some type of issue with him. Why can't he love me and only me? I have given him all of me. I mean this man has explored places that no other man will ever explore with me. But he was able to because I trusted him with my feelings, my body and my heart. Why was I not enough for him?

I know that I was wrong for sleeping with Rico. But he expressed such a desire for me. He made me feel like Ken used to when I first met him. I know that it was only physical but I want to pretend that he wanted me for me. I can't place blame for my actions on someone else but I almost want to say Ken made me do it.

I get so tired of covering up his dirt. I know he cheats. I know he entertains his female clients in unconventional ways. He thinks I'm naïve to his games but I'm far from naïve. The killer to that is I've only wised up since I've been with him. He has made me a superior investigator. He has made my heart cold with insecurity and distrust. It was him that pushed me to where I am now. I'm sick and tired of being sick and tired.

Then you have Rico. He came into my life just a few days ago and things have been buck wild ever since. He is gorgeous but so is my man. He rocked my world but my man is capable of doing the same thing. We share the same interest, well Kenyon and I don't. Rico respects and admires the reputation that I have built for myself in corporate America. Kenyon has disrespected me by parading around with these hoes like my reputation for being one of the hardest working women in the advertising business means shit to him. My colleagues have seen him so many times. I was so embarrassed, making up lies and excuses for his behavior.

As I peered out into the darkness, my room illuminated by the lights of the City that never sleeps, I let my mind travel to my future. I needed to focus. I had been assigned the project of a lifetime and all I could think about was men.

I decided from that point on, that this was about me. Sequoia Nicole Johnson. No one else. I'm going to continue to make my mark in this coldhearted city. I will make a name for myself that speaks volumes. I will demand respect from anyone I encounter. Business or Personal. I'm sick and tired of being sick and tired.

I turned on my phone and checked my messages. The familiar computerized voice told me I had three new messages. The first one was from my Mom, wondering where the hell I was. Why I hadn't gone to work today? And when would I return her calls? "Damn Mom, can I get a break? Just one day," I said out loud to the empty room. The next one was from Nika. Just checking on me. I shuddered when I thought of the nightmare I'd had earlier but then shook those thoughts. My girl was low down but I know that was one line that she wouldn't cross. At least I hoped. The next message came in at 12:30 and was from a private caller because the computerized voice didn't recite the number. My heart fluttered when I heard Rico's voice:

"Hey pretty lady. I know you're probably getting some much deserved rest right now but I wanted you to know that I was thinking about you. I enjoyed myself immensely last night but I wanted you to know if you're worried about what I'm thinking, rest assured they are only good thoughts. It's been a while since a woman has affected me the way that you have, physically and mentally. You are the most beautiful, intelligent and hard working woman that I've ever met. I'm not bullshitting either. I need that in my life. I'm not trying to push you. I'm a man of patience. I'll wait for what I know is good for me. Missed you at work today, I was working full speed ahead on the project. When you come in tomorrow maybe we can go over some of my drafts. Sweet dreams."

I listened to the message over and over again. I finally erased it because I knew I would replay it again. Why was he fucking with my head? I got back in the bed and listened to the emptiness in the room. The quiet was relaxing. I liked to listen to nothing sometimes. I let the quietness of the room rock me back to sleep.

He Said…She Said

Chapter 11

He Said…

7 woke up to the scent of Koi's perfume. It was 5:30 am and there was no alarm clock going off. No coffee brewing. I noticed no steam flowing from the shower and when I stepped onto the cold marble tiles in the bathroom it hit me. All the things that made this loft feel like a home were gone. The reason I think we chose this place was because there were no walls. Just like there were no walls or barriers in our relationship until now. I have never known Koi to stay out all night and I've definitely never known her to skip work. But hell, I was starting to think that I really don't know her the way I once thought I did.

I arrived at my office a little earlier than usual because I really couldn't stand being at home. Everything there reminded me of Koi. The kitchen because that was the first place we made love, the living room area because that's where she used to work on her crossword puzzles and the bedroom because that is where I used to hold her and where we used to wrestle. I would let her win because I love her being on top of me.

So I got here a little early to get away from all that and also to prepare for my meeting with Ms. Roberts. I was ready to show her what I had planned for her money and how I was going to make her even wealthier than she already was. I saw Shanice at her desk when I got off the elevator and had to remind myself to be a professional. "I hope this woman ain't tripping today because I can't take her attitude. As I got closer to my office I saw her look up. "Good morning Mr. Burnett. I see you wanted the worm today referring to my early arrival.

"Yeah I thought it was time for me to get back to doing what I love to do, making people money."

"I think your going to be really surprised by who's in your office and by the way, about the other night."

"Before you even say it, it shouldn't have happened right?"

"No. Wrong it should have happened. I'm just sorry I met you when you're trying to be a good man. Hey, but all you wanted was a good…."

"Stop that." I said with a smile because I saw the old Shanice creeping back into the conversation. I grabbed my mail and messages and walked into my office, trying to remember whose appointment I had forgotten and there she was. I couldn't believe the nerve of this woman. Kim was sitting on the edge of my desk looking like she wanted to kill me.

She Said…

I woke up feeling pretty good. I'd actually slept soundly once I'd fallen off to sleep. I showered and cursed myself for not bringing my flat irons. I pulled my long mane to the back and rolled it into a bun at the nape of my neck. I put on my killer suit with a slate gray blouse and my Ferragamo heels. I topped off my look with the Gucci frames that Ken hated. He said they made me look like a nerd. I think they made me look intelligent, see the differences I'm talking about?

I ordered the personal chef who almost magically appeared at 7 am to make me a Western omelet with hash browns. It was delicious. I was ready to start my day.

As I pulled out of the parking structure I should have turned left to head towards the Reed agency but something literally pulled my car to the right. Something told me that I should go to Ken's office. I decided then that I would go and talk to him.

Just days ago, I felt like he was my soul mate. I had put up with some bullshit but I know in my heart that I love him. He is worth working with. I want to make my relationship work. I should be ashamed for letting someone come into my life and turn it upside down. Rico is a brilliant artist and a wonderful lover but I had to separate the two. I needed to change our relationship back to business only. I'm confident that I can do this. I mean I'm a grown ass woman who has been responsible for marketing fortune 500 companies, making their products or services appeal to the general public. I know all about business and it should always come before pleasure.

That was it! I'm going to make this shit work if it kills me. Ken is the man for me and I will make him see that I'm more than the woman for him.

I pulled in the parking structure and greeted the security guard. He let me pull in and I pulled into my Dad's reserved parking spot. I figured he was somewhere having breakfast now anyway. Besides I was only going to be a minute. Unless my appeal for the relationship turned into another love session! I smiled at the thought.

I listened to the elevator music and wondered why everyone always dogged it out. I happened to like the Bee Gees song that was presently playing. Half way up, the elevator stopped and picked up an older white woman. I bid her a good morning and she ignored me. "Whatever," I said to myself. I refused to let anyone spoil my mood.

I stepped off at my floor and turned to her and said, "Have a good day." She frowned as the elevator doors closed.

He Said…

I couldn't believe this bitch had the balls to show up in my office like we're old friends or something. The nerve of this crazy woman. Dressed to impress in her pants suit that hugged her body like a glove and her Jil Sander boots showed that she was there to show me what I was missing out on by not being with her. But my heart is with Koi and with that in mind I was furious not only to see her in my office but also at the fact my know it all secretary let her ass in, an issue that I will be taking up with her ass as soon as I get this perplexed woman out of my office.

As I walked in I closed the door to my office but didn't close my blinds to the picture window looking out at my secretary because I didn't want Kim to say I put my hands on her. I needed witnesses this time.

"Look Kim, I don't know why you're here but I think you should leave right now. I'm going to set my brief case down and go to wash my hands and when I come out I'd like you to be gone or I'm going to call security. So why don't you make my day a little easier and just leave on your own."

"Leave? Baby why would I do that? You're the one who drove me to this. You told me that I was the woman you loved and now you can threaten to just put me out your damn office like I'm some bitch off the street!" She said with her voice going up like she was trying to make a scene.

"This is not a threat Kim, it's a promise. Look I don't have time for this, just get your ass out of here. Haven't you done enough damage? Shit you had the damn police pick me up from here, my damn job! In front of my co- workers! You didn't even consider my reputation."

"Your reputation? You son of a bitch, what about my heart? You made me believe you were my man then out of no where you leave me for some church-going bitch that barely fucks you."

"See that's your problem. You're concerned about shit that doesn't have anything to do with you. I don't need to hear this shit. You need to just leave, get the hell out."

Kim had hit a nerve. My dumb ass, pillow talking told her little things like Koi not wanting to have sex with me or about when she was too tired to have sex.

"Did I hit a sore spot? Your little angel can't please you or wouldn't huh? Why can't we just go back to being friends with benefits Ken? Can't you see how much I love you?"

"Kim, you don't know the meaning of love. Look, it's over between me and you. Whatever it was, it's over. Now I need you to get the hell out."

She Said…

As the elevator doors opened I saw Shanice, the chick Ken had introduced me to at the restaurant the other night. I could tell that she recognized me as well, from the look on her face or was that surprise?

"Hi Shanice. Is Kenyon in his office?" I asked. Then I saw him walk past the window that overlooks his secretary's desk.

"Oh I see him. I'll see myself in," I said before she could answer. Though she looked all flustered anyway. What was her problem?

I opened Kenyon's office door and was immediately met by two sets of eyes, both filled with anger. His changed from anger to surprise. Hers stayed steady at anger.

"Hey Ken. I didn't know you had a client. I had something to talk to you about. I have a few minutes so I'll go see if my Dad has made it in yet." I turned to walk out the door but his "client" said, "I'm not a client."

I stopped in my tracks because I could tell from her tone that it was some shit in the game. I turned around to face them both.

Ken immediately began to stammer. "Ye..Yes, she is."

"No, I'm not," she said.

"Ok, well who is she?" I asked Ken.

"I'm standing right here, you can ask me," she said defiantly with her shoulders squared.

Me, not ever being one to step away from a challenge, walked over to her and asked, "Who are you?"

Ken rushed over to us and grabbed my hand. "Baby, we were just finishing up here. Why don't you have Shanice get us some coffee and I'll be right with you."

"Hell, no. What the hell is going on here?" I asked them both.

"Sequoia, I'm Kim, Kenyon's fuck partner for the last six months. It's a pleasure to finally meet the Ice Princess."

"Ice Princess? Fuck Partner?" I looked at Kenyon for some answers before I proceeded to beat the shit out of this bitch.

"Koi. Don't listen to her. She's crazy. I was just about to have her put out."

"You're a damn lie Kenyon. Ain't shit crazy about me. Tell her the truth for once, you asshole." Kim screamed.

"Baby..." Kenyon pleaded.

I held my hand to his face to silence him. He could tell from the look on my face that I meant business. I stepped up to this bitch that had literally crushed my plans for renewed happiness with my man and said, "In any other instance I would beat your ass for disrespecting me but you get a free pass today because I really think you just don't know any better. But you aren't committed to me, he is or at least I thought he was. So you can have his ass."

I started to walk to the door and Ken grabbed my arm. I snatched away from him and told him, "Don't put your fucking hands on me, ever. You've fucked over me for the last time." I walked towards the door where Shanice was now standing. She must have come to the door when she heard the ruckus coming from inside his office. She gave me a look of pity but I ice-grilled her ass because as far as I was concerned she was probably fucking him too.

Just as we were shoulder to shoulder I said, "If you value your job you better be on your best behavior. Don't forget whose last name is on the front door, bitch." I walked to the elevator which, thank God, was open and waiting for me like a pair of comforting arms. I turned and took in the scene that I was leaving to etch it permanently into my memory and the elevator doors closed.

He Said…She Said

Chapter 12

He Said…

I walked into the loft not knowing exactly what I would find. The smell of jasmine hit me as soon as I got off the elevator. Kem was the sound that serenaded the candle lit loft, there was a sense of calmness that filled the air and I kept saying to myself that everything was going to be okay. Koi is going to believe that the woman she encountered in my office was some crazy ex that had been stalking me. Even though Kim hadn't only said we'd been fucking but also mentioned that I'd told her that Koi and I weren't making love at all. Yeah right. Who the hell was I trying to convince? I had no idea how I was going to get myself off this sinking ship.

I walked into the bedroom and noticed that all my stuff was still in place. All my suits were still hung neatly in the closet. My watches were still in a perfect row on the chest. Maybe Koi was taking what happened today better than I'd expected.

I walked into the bathroom and saw the steam from the bath tub and the candle on the counter of the sink. She looked so peaceful that I didn't think she knew I was there, until after a few minutes of watching her soak her problems away in the jetted bath tub she said without moving a muscle, "Ken you really hurt me today and I don't think I'm going to be able to forgive you this time."

"Baby, I understand but if you'll let me explain I'm sure we can work this out. I haven't fucked with that woman in a really long time."

"But the thing is you did fuck with her. She didn't make that up. Ken you shared our intimate secrets with another woman. You put my business in the street, shit you put our business in the street. Then you had the nerve to even let this bitch know where you work. So she shows up at your office and

93

shows her ass so everyone in the office, including my family, knows that my man is not only cheating on me but has the audacity to do it at my fathers company. I must admit Ken you got balls."

"Koi I'm sorry. Just give me a minute to explain my side."

"Your side? I don't want to hear your side. I just want you to go. I want you out of my home."

"This is my home too. You need to just calm down."

"Look Ken, I love you so much and I really don't want the last time we talk to be a fight or another lie so why don't you be a man and leave. I will send you your things."

I found myself with an overnight bag and a garment bag with three suits at the elevator when I heard Koi say, "Leave the keys on the counter please." With those words I knew it was over. She'd never even opened her eyes or raised her voice and that was three weeks ago. To say that I'm sad would be a terrible understatement. I feel like I've not only lost my future wife but my best friend.

Since the break up I not only been staying at Colin's house I've been working my ass off trying to do whatever it take to keep Koi off my mind. I've been working on Ms. Robert's portfolio a lot lately. I took the money she gave me and put it in a few good stocks but I hit the jackpot when I put her in this concrete company called Dolby construction. They'd won the contract to have their concrete used for the entire pavement in Iraq after the war. When I bought the stock it was $3.67 per share it had grown over 80% since they'd won the bid. I'd bought her nine hundred thousand shares! Needless to say she was extremely grateful. She wanted to thank me at her birthday party. I really didn't want to go but I figured it would take my mind off of Koi. A party was really the last thing on my mind but it was for work, so I had to do what I had to do.

She Said…

I was devastated, to say the least. I stayed in the bathtub until I resembled a prune. The warm water was so comforting. I finally dragged myself out of the tub and wrapped up in my robe. My hair was soaked. My eyes were red and puffy. I looked a mess. I crawled into my huge bed alone. I was so hurt. But then I felt those stabbing pangs of guilt. Who was I to judge Ken? I too had committed the same crime he had, he just didn't know it. I tried to justify my indiscretion by counting the numerous times that I'd been on the short end of the stick with Kenyon and his hoes. I still felt bad but this just convinced me that we really weren't meant to be.

The next day, I woke up to an empty loft. I started my day out with a prayer asking that the Lord forgive me for my sins and grant me the strength and serenity to move on peacefully. I felt better after I finished praying. I gave it over to God who had helped so many times before when I'd knelt before him asking him for strength. I knew if no one else could work this mess out, He definitely could and would. With that, I dressed and prepared to throw myself full throttle into the "Gym shoe project."

When I arrived at the office, I called a meeting. As everyone filed into the conference room, I noticed Rico and Sandy walking in together. I smiled and rushed them both in.

"Good morning, everyone. Thank you all for holding down the fort yesterday. I feel much better, for those of you who were concerned. I'm back and ready to tackle this monstrous project. I cannot even begin to explain the possibilities and opportunities that will arise from a top notch product for this project. I am and have always been a team player. I will let you know that I stand to gain a huge compensation package from this if we pull this off or I should say when we pull this off. I promise you that we all, this whole team, will benefit from that compensation package. We are a team. There is no "I" in team. If

I win, we all win. So I expect your best work. I will not accept anything less than your best. If I feel you are slacking, you will be removed from this project. WE don't have time to play around with this. NO distractions. Personal or Professional. Take your Vitamin C tablets, your Echinacea or whatever you need to. I have cases of the energy drink Red Bull in the refrigerator. I'm not playing people. Let's get to work!! I will speak to you all individually throughout the day to get a grasp on my expectations and your individual responsibilities. Have a great day!!"

Sequoia watched as they all filed out and spoke in nervous chatter amongst themselves. That is everyone but Rico.

"Hey you. It's good to see you back. I know you got my message last night."

"I did. Thanks for being concerned. I feel much better. About the other night…"

"Sequoia, we don't have to talk about that. We're grown ups. What happened, happened. I can't say I didn't enjoy it and that I don't hope it happens again, but I'm ok with it," he said.

"Yeah, I think I would much rather let it be, at least for now. I've got a lot going on and could really use a friend right now."

"Then friend it is. I can handle that, at least I'll try," he joked.

"Thanks Rico. Now let's get to work."

Chapter 13

He Said…

I must admit standing here in my black Armani suit and Prada shoes, I'm looking like a winner. I'm glad I can hide the way I'm feeling and not show it because I would be one of the ugliest men in the world.

I arrived at the Pure club a little after eleven. I'd heard a lot about this club and it was living up to the hype. I'd already peeped a few members of the hip hop community as well as a few A-list actors partying in VIP. I'm more than impressed with what I see in this up scale sports bar. Plasma televisions on every wall all tuned into the Knicks game, patrons throwing back spirits and cheering their home team on.

After a few minutes I was greeted by Tanisha with a bottle of Cristal in her right hand and two glasses in her left she shouted out at me, "Baby we're going to party tonight!"

With a shy smile I nodded my head in agreement and said to myself, "I'm out of here by 2 o'clock." Before I could utter a word she had grabbed me by the arm and whisked me away to a crowd of her friends and family. I wasn't really paying them any attention when I noticed the guy, Rico that I'd seen Koi with. He was standing really close to another lady that I'm sure I'd seen at Koi's company Christmas party last year. Even though I'd vowed to let that situation go, I was right back at it instantly trying to figure out what was really going on with this cat Rico. I know in my heart that when I saw him with Koi, it wasn't as innocent as she wanted me to believe. To see him here with one of her coworkers, hugging and whispering in her ear almost made me happy. At least I knew he wasn't concentrating solely on my girl.

I just can't figure out what Koi sees in this guy. He is the exact opposite of any man she's ever dated and a coworker at that. I can't get past that because Koi wouldn't even date someone that went to her school, let alone someone she worked with.

I watched them for a minute until I saw Tanisha waving me back over to where she stood. I'd almost made it back over to her when I noticed who she was standing there with. It was Nika.

"Hey Ken, this is my good friend Nika. Nika this is my friend and financial advisor Ken."

Nika interrupted her by saying, "I know Ken very well. He used to date my girl Koi."

"Used to date her? As in…not anymore? Ken why didn't you tell me that you and your woman weren't an item any more?" purred Tanisha.

"Well I guess because I didn't want everyone to know my damn business. I'm a man. I can hurt in silence." I said looking at Nika.

"Hurt? Ken you're the one who hurt my girl. She loved you and you embarrassed the hell out of her."

"Nika, you don't know the whole story so why don't you just let it go."

"I wish I could, but she's at home sick over your ass and you out partying like you don't have a care in the world," she yelled.

"Look you two. I don't want this here at my party. I'm celebrating my birthday and the millions that you've made me and Nika we've been cool as long as I've been living here so just let whatever problems ya'll have go for the night and go back to being mad in the morning," said Tanisha.

"I'm too old to be arguing in the club, Nika. Go ahead and enjoy yourself Tanisha. I'm going over to the bar." I turned and walked away. This was too much for me.

I turned around to see Tanisha dragging Nika over to a crowd of New Jersey Net basketball players all standing by the free bar. "She must really know Nika well. If she wanted to shut Nika up, show her where the men with money are and she would forget whatever it was that was bothering her," I thought to myself.

I spent half the night people watching. I watched Nika smiling at anyone 6'5" or taller. It seemed like she knew one of these guys had to be the pay day she been looking for. I also kept close watch on Rico and Koi's coworker. I saw Rico and his date walk over to the bar and decided to say hello. I hadn't quite formulated a plan, but I would ad lib if I had to. The need to find out what was going on with him and Koi had suddenly become very urgent.

As I made my move over to them, for some strange reason I couldn't remember the name that I'd told him at the Tonic jazz bar to save my life. I really wasn't sure if I wanted him to know who I was yet and besides I wasn't sure if the chick would remember me and that would have really blown my cover.

I had an idea. I knew it was sneaky but I asked the drunken Tanisha could I use her phone and I text a message to Koi.

Hey Sequoia-I was just thinking about you. If you're thinking about me, call me. I will understand if you can't because your man is around. -From you know who

After sending the text, I watched Rico like a hawk and just like I expected he looked at his phone but didn't answer it. That right there let me know that he was more than just a friend to my woman. But how could I find out just how much more with out invading Koi's privacy? I'd agreed to leave her alone but I needed her in my life. I quickly abandoned the idea of speaking to him.

Seeing De'Rico look at his phone had me heated so I decided to just go home, I said my goodbyes to Tanisha and her friends. As I was leaving I stopped in front of Nika and asked her to tell Koi that I'd been thinking about her. This hood rat scoffed and turned her back on me.

I had almost made it to the door when I felt a tap on my shoulder.

"What's up Keith?"

I almost kept walking but I recognized the voice. I turned to see Rico standing behind me, thank goodness by himself.

"Oh, what's up man? I was just about to get out of here," I said.

"Man the party is just starting. You know Tanisha can throw a helluva party. You flying solo tonight? Where's my man Colin?" he asked me.

"Oh, I think he is chilling with your cousin. I only came tonight because Tanisha is a client."

"You must be the topnotch financial planner she has been raving about. She gave everybody your card. I might have to check you out. I'm working on a big project now that should be a huge windfall for everyone working on it. I'm working with one of the best Creative Directors in town. Yeah, I'm definitely going to look you up later," Rico said.

I thought to myself, "You'll be hearing from me sooner than that nigga." "Alright, well good luck on that project. Hit me up when you need to. By the way, no disrespect but that's a nice looking young lady you have with you." I slyly slid in.

"Oh, Sandy? She's cool. I can introduce you if you want. She's pressing me so damn hard, I can't stand it. I was trying to get this other chick out of the house but she isn't feeling good, so Sandy volunteered herself. I didn't want to come alone so I brought her. But she's all yours if you want her. I got my eye on something else," he responded.

I was so damn close to knocking his ass out, I had to excuse myself. "Naw, I'm good. I'll see you around."

When I finally got to my truck I was out of breath and feeling very nauseated. Something has got to give.

I got back to Colin's place and decided that I was looking for my own place tomorrow and would stop driving myself crazy about Koi. If we are meant to be she will be back. Who am I kidding? I need her back. Right now. Today. Forever.

He Said…She Said

Chapter 14

She Said…

I was almost pissed that I hadn't accepted Rico's invitation to some party he'd been invited to. Here I was again sitting in the house drowning in my sorrows. I hadn't heard from Ken and that was a good thing. I was so depressed I probably would have given in if he'd called because I wanted the pain to stop. I wasn't in the mood for a party. But I was surprised that Rico had text me. I sent him back a short message saying I hoped he was having a good time and I would just see him tomorrow.

I was feeling guilty about my feelings for him. Over the course of a few days, I had found myself comparing him and Ken. All the things that I loved about Ken in the beginning were all in place with Rico. Then there were all the things that we had in common. We were both artist, we loved Jazz, and our bodies melted together like a piece of ceramic art. It was impossible for me to just forget about the other night. Try as I might to push him as far away as possible, Rico was under my skin.

I was laughing at the little innuendo that he'd left in his text "I'll understand if you can't call because your man is there." If he only knew. I hadn't told anyone except Nika that I'd asked Ken to leave, including my parents. My mother would be devastated. As far as she was concerned I should have been married with two kids, two years ago. I guess I was chopped minced meat to anyone other than Ken. Huh, if only she knew. I just wasn't ready to face the million and one questions that I knew would be asked.

I woke up with a clear head. I decided today would be a denim and ponytail day. I'd planned on being in the office all day so I needed to be comfortable. I stopped at Starbucks to get a latte. I remember Rico having an Irish Crème coffee at Justin's so I picked him one up too. I felt good when I walked into the office. I stopped by Rico's desk to give him his coffee.

"Well looks like you may have had too much fun," I joked referring to his unshaven face and the way he was leaning on his desk.

"Yeah, I may have pushed my drink limit. I blame it all on you because if you'd come like I'd ask you to, I wouldn't have drank myself silly. But I needed liquor in my system to calm my nerves because Sandy was driving me crazy! You talk about two faced. You would never imagine from her cool, all business attitude here, how she gets with a few drinks in her."

"Oh, I've seen Sandy at a few after work functions. I didn't warn you I just figured you'd find out for yourself. So did she jump your bones in the car?" I joked.

"Funny that you would say that, I had to swat her hand like five times on the way to the party! Then after the drinks she was wild woman! I was trying to pawn her off on this guy I knew. He wasn't having it though. That reminds me, if I can find his card I'll make you a copy because he is supposed to be the top of the line in financial advisors," said Rico as he popped his second set of Advil that morning.

"I don't need help managing my pennies. Maybe when we complete this project but for right now, I'm cool." I patted his back and immediately felt electric shocks flow through my body. "Note to self – No touching," I said to myself. "I feel your pain on the hangover but nonetheless you better get it together. You've got a lot of work to do."

"Yeah, yeah," he said as he laid his head on his desk.
I walked out of his cubicle and bumped into Sandy. "Good morning, Sandy."

I chuckled at the thought of him fighting her off. I went into my office and shut the door.

I plowed through my emails and checked my voicemail, still no Ken. I pushed the thought of him staying with another woman out of my head and began my day.

Though my biggest project was the "Gym Shoe Project," which had become known around the office as the "GP," I still had other projects to work on.

I was listening to some tapes of candidates to do some voiceover work on a radio spot for one of our clients. I was just about falling to sleep when Mr. Reed knocked on my door.

"Good morning Sequoia. I wanted to give you these tickets to the Knicks game. I was at dinner with Isaiah last night and he gave them to me for promo but it looks like you could use some fun in your life," he placed the tickets on my desk.

'Thanks Mr. Reed. You're right about that. I appreciate you thinking of me."

"No problem. You're my number one girl. I am happy that you're here. Whatever I can do to make sure you stay here, I'm gonna do it. And let me tell you this, whatever it is that is bothering you will work out. I won't pester you for details but I've noticed you seem a little down and I've never known you to show it at work. So I know it's something serious but you're a good woman and if you have faith it will all work out."

'Thanks Mr. Reed. I'm sure it will," I said with tears in my eyes.

"Ok, enough of that. Enjoy the game," he smiled and closed my door. I had just switched the tape on again but there was another knock at my door. Rico walked in looking much better than before.

"Hey when you get a chance can you take a look at some of the models I selected? I have a few in line to come in but I'm on the fence about these two."

"Yeah, no problem. It's gonna be a minute because I have to find a voice for this commercial. I'm already a day behind schedule. Hey are you busy tonight? Mr. Reed gave me suite tickets for the Knicks. I figured if you weren't busy maybe you could go with me."

"For sure. You think we'll finish up here in enough time?" he asked.

"Did you forget I'm the boss? We close up shop when I say so," I laughed.

"Well alright Big Mama. Well let me get back to work so we can get out of here," he said.

He closed my door and I sat back in my chair. "Yeah I think I just might be ok."

Chapter 15

He Said…

I spent most of the morning searching for an apartment. Tanisha called at the crack of dawn to reiterate that she had given any and everybody who she thought would benefit from my services my business card. That was cool but I wondered if she thought since she was throwing business my way, I just might throw some dick her way. That ain't happening though. Especially since I know that she knows the biggest mouth in New York. That would be right up Nika's alley. I could just see her blowing up Koi's phone, email and any other way she could get to her.

Tanisha was finally finished giving me the rundown on all the people I should expect to call me. I waited patiently before I asked for a referral for an apartment broker. She eagerly gave me a name and number. Again I felt there was an ulterior motive but what the hell, at this point I really had nothing to lose.

"Yeah, Kenyon. James will set you up right in the center of it all. You need to be in the mix. Besides he could probably use a consultation with you as well. Maybe you guys can trade services? As a matter fact he is going to the Knicks game with me tonight, I'll introduce you two, if you take these two floor seat tickets off my hands."

I almost fell off my bed. I'd been to the games and had pretty good seats, but floor seats? Man, I was there!

"That would be cool. What time is the game?"

"Tip off is at 8 o'clock. I'll leave your tickets at will call. You need to get out and get that girl off your mind," said Tanisha.

"I don't know if that's possible Tanisha but I appreciate the tickets," I said as I locked Colin's door and headed to the office.

When I arrived at the office Shanice was at her desk looking nice in a cream colored top and her hair pulled back in a ponytail. I spoke and took my messages from her. Still no word from Koi. I knew she was really mad but I had expected her to at least call me and cuss me out.

I buzzed Shanice and told her to come to my office. I couldn't help but notice the total package that was standing in my doorway. She had on a beautifully fitting cream skirt to match the blouse and a pair of Tod heels. I probably wouldn't have known the name of her shoes if Koi wasn't such a shoe fanatic.

I regained my focus and said, "Shanice I need you to order 50 dozen of the most beautiful roses and lilies that you can find."

Shanice frantically took notes.

"Sign the card *'Don't think for one minute that I am not thinking of you every second of every day that I have been away from you. You stay on my mind. – Ken'*" I instructed. "I need them to be delivered today and also get Colin on the phone for me."

"No problem Ken, I mean Mr. Burnett. Is there anything else I can do for you?" she asked.

"No, but thanks for your help," I said absently as I browsed through my messages. I noticed my sister had been calling all morning.

"By the way Ms. Roberts left a number for you and said I should set something up for you."

"Oh yeah. See if you can get me in around 11 today."

"I will," she said with what seemed like an attitude but that was typical of Shanice.

I was in deep thought about my situation with Koi when my buzzer sounded, signaling me that Colin was on the line.

"What's up Colin," I asked.

"Nothing man. On my way to grab a bite. What's good?"

"I've got tickets to the game tonight, floor seats, and wanted to know if you wanted to go?"

"For sho. You know they play the Piston's tonight. Damn how did you get those tickets? That game has been sold out."

"One of my clients gave them to me," I said absently.

"Damn. Well thank your client for me. I'll be home by six but you know I gotta go hit Foot Locker to get me a Billups Jersey."

"Man, are you serious? If you and Spike Lee get into it, you're on your own," I laughed.

"Man, I would…" I cut him off before he could finish.

"I gotta go man. Just be home by six."

"Alright."

I was laughing as I dialed the number that my sister had left but Koi was not far from my mind. This had become the norm for me.

Shanice paced back and forth in front of her desk. "I can't believe this soft ass nigga is still crying over that bitch. I bent over backwards to impress his ass. I even went out and bought these expensive ass shoes because I saw her ass in a pair before. Oooh! I am so pissed." She sat back at her desk and looked up the number to the florist the company used.

"Hello, can you please send 30 dozen roses and lilies to Sequoia Johnson at the Reed Agency. Sign the card, from Ken."

She chuckled to herself, "The other 20 dozen are paying for these damn shoes. He'll never know!"

He Said…She Said

Chapter 16

She Said…

I must say I was surprised when the first 5 dozen of flowers were delivered but when the guy kept coming back into my office, I was floored. It looked like a funeral parlor in my office. I knew immediately they were from Ken because he is always so over the top with everything he does.

I had the whole office in my area by the time the last dozen were placed wherever they could fit. There was chatter of how they wished they'd had a man like mine. How long it had been since they'd had flowers delivered at work. I wanted to put them all out and cry but I had to front and be polite. Rico came to my office door and just shook his head and smiled. He walked away before I could say anything.

After I fielded all the questions I could stand, I was finally alone again. I wondered would it be wrong to email him a thank you message. I just wasn't ready to hear his voice yet. Unfortunately he still had that power over me. I would melt like butter if he said the right thing. I decided that I would send him a thank you card tomorrow.

I was ready for the game. They were playing the Pistons who happened to be the hottest team in the NBA. I loved my Knicks but the time that I spent in Detroit during college had turned me into a die hard Pistons fan. I closed up shop and stopped by Rico's desk before I left.

He gave me "the look" as I approached his desk.

"What??" I asked even though I knew exactly what he was thinking.

"That dude is playing hardball Sequoia. He wants his woman back," said Rico as he worked on a logo design.

"Ok, and so? What does that have to do with me or you? Ken had his chance and fucked up time and time again. If I'm not worried, why are you?" I asked.

"I'm not worried. You are, no matter what you say. But I ain't tripping. I just see he ain't going nowhere without a fight. That's cool too. I trained at Kronk's gym," he joked.

"Whatever. We're just friends anyway. Remember? So there won't be any fighting, got it?"

"Umm-hmmm," he said with that sly look again.

"I'll pick you up around six or I can park my car at your place and we'll take a cab to avoid the traffic. Ok?"

"Sounds good to me, buddy old pal." Said Rico.

"You're not funny," I slapped him playfully and walked to the lobby. I signed out and headed to my car.

The drive home was insane. There were all kinds of accidents and traffic jams. By the time I reached the loft I was fit to be tied. I threw my briefcase down in the foyer and kicked off my shoes. I thought I heard music and my heart skipped a beat.

"I know he's not in here." I said speaking of Ken. I knew I had collected his keys so technically this would be considered breaking and entering. I charged through the loft to the bedroom, half expecting and half hoping it was him. At least I could curse him out again to relieve some of the stress and pressure. I pushed open the door and was so disappointed when I heard my alarm clock blaring Keisha Cole's "I should have cheated." I had forgotten to turn the alarm off this morning.

I sat down on my bed and laughed at myself. "Look at you. You don't want him here but you do want him here. You don't want to be with him but you miss him terribly. What is really going on with you Sequoia Johnson?" I asked myself.

I slid across the hardwood floor and walked into my closet. What the hell was I going to wear? I knew it was going to be jeans but which ones? I settled on a pair of dark denim with the washed out front. The hems were kind of frayed like I like them so they fell down over my boots perfectly. I topped it off with a black fitted cowl neck and redid my ponytail and spiked it a little. I put on the gigantic pair of solitaire earrings Ken had bought me for Valentine's Day one year. I swear I could contend with Nelly with the size of these babies. I threw on a few white gold bangles and topped it with my Chinchilla vest. I changed my Coach bag and put my valuables into my Chanel bag and was on my way out the door when the phone rang.

I almost stopped to answer but I figured whoever it was would call my cell phone if it was important. I pulled the gate to the elevator down and was one my way.

When I got to Rico's he was ready thank goodness. He led me into his living room and offered me a drink, which I eagerly accepted. He was looking so damn good, I found myself staring. He had on LRG blue jeans with the tan washed look and a LRG jacket that was army green and tan with the matching green Air Force Ones with the tan swoosh. He was very fly to say the least. I threw the drink down and ask for another one. "Friends. We are just friends," I kept saying over and over in my mind.

We talked about the project and he told me about his family during the cab ride to the arena. He also told me that he had a daughter that lived in Jersey but her mother wouldn't let him see her. I didn't ask why, I figured he'd tell me when he was ready to.

He paid the cab driver and we pushed our way through the crowd into the arena. It was a mad house! The pre-game activities had started and the crowd was really into it. It seemed like we'd stepped into a club. Music was blaring; people were standing at the mini-bars stationed throughout the arena socializing. I stopped and got another drink and then we found our seats. I didn't know the seats were floor seats. I hadn't even looked at the tickets until we showed the usher. Rico was tripping.

"Damn. This is right on time. Floor seats?! I'm tripping," he said.

"I know. I didn't know we would be right in the mix," I laughed.

We got settled and I had just swallowed a gulp of my drink when I saw Ken and Colin walking our way!

He Said…

The atmosphere in the Garden was just like I thought it would be. The upper echelon were here to watch the Pistons, last year's Eastern conference champs, play against their old coach Larry Brown and the New York Knicks. I couldn't wait until tip off. Spike Lee was in his normal seat right near Jay Z, who was part owner of the New Jersey Nets. I mean everybody was here and I couldn't believe I had these seats.

"Man, that's Ben Wallace." Colin said excitedly.

"I know Colin."

"That's Maurice Taylor."

"Colin I know who's who stop being groupie." I said jokingly but was dead serious. He was already on his way to working my nerves.

"We're going to have a ball. The Pistons are going to kick the Knicks' ass and then I'm going to go home and make a few calls to get me some bomb ass pussy tonight."

"Colin you swear you getting some ass. You still worried about Chanelle and as long as she's around that's the only ass you getting."

"You got jokes, huh? At least she ain't here with another nigga."

"What's that supposed to mean?"

"Meaning, isn't that Sequoia right there standing with Chanelle cousin Rico?"

"What the fuck?" were the only words I remember saying before I started making my way over to them. I made my way past all the celebrities and walked right up to Koi.

"Koi, can I talk to you for a minute?" I asked, trying to remain calm.

"Hey Keith, what's going on man. I didn't know you knew my woman Sequoia."

"Woman? Keith? Rico, this is my ex Ken. Where did you get Keith from?" Sequoia said with the most confused look on her face.

"He got it from what I told him and what the heck you mean your woman?"

"My woman means exactly that."

"Koi it's like that ma? You kicking it with the help now?"

"Ken come off it. You're causing a scene we can talk about this later." Said Koi as she tried to walk past me.

"There is nothing to talk about ya'll are done. Right?" asked Rico.

"Please Rico, let me handle this. Ken really there isn't anything to talk about. Besides, I came here to watch the game not rehash our dysfunctional relationship. We can talk about this tomorrow."

"Tomorrow! What the fuck do you mean tomorrow?" By this time the security was approaching fast. Colin grabbed me by the shoulder and said "Come on man." I couldn't take my eyes of Koi and I couldn't look at any one else because I didn't want them to see the hurt in my eyes.

"Excuse me is there a problem over here?" asked the guy with the red blazer with security on it.

"No sir, there's not a problem. We're on our way back to our seats." Colin said.

"Okay, can I see your tickets?" Robo-cop asked as I stood there in a daze, looking like a damn fool.

"Yo Ken let me get the tickets." I heard him but I didn't respond. Everything seemed to be going in slow motion around me. I heard the roar of the crowd and even though they were rallying for their home team, it seemed like they were all laughing at me. I stood there watching as Rico guided my woman to their seats holding her elbow. Not even noticing that I was now surrounded by four little white guys and one huge black guy.

"Ken can you give these guys the tickets please."

"Yea man here," I said as I handed the tickets to him. "I'm sorry Colin. Take the keys to the truck, I'm leaving."

"Man you don't have to leave. How are you going to get home?"

"I'm going to take the train. I'll see you when you get home."

"Naw man, I'll come with you. Fuck the game."

"Thanks man, but I need to think. Stay here and enjoy the game. I need to be alone for a while. I'll get at you later."

I made my way out of the Garden and back into the streets of New York. Where I was going? Your guess is good as mine.

She Said…

I couldn't believe this shit. In an arena with 70,000 seats, I just so happen to be in the same damn section at the same damn time, with Ken. I swear if it wasn't for bad luck, I wouldn't have any luck at all. What made it worse was why the hell would Rico say that I was his woman? He was out of line. I was mad but flattered at the same time. Then what the hell was that "Keith" shit? I just knew Colin had something to do with that. He is always in the mix.

Rico was watching the game like nothing had happened but I could tell he had an attitude. This was too much for me. All in a weeks time I'd cheated on my man, found out that I'd been cheated on and then been busted but not really busted by my ex-boyfriend. "Boy, I should write a book," I thought to myself.

So I tried to concentrate on the game like Rico. I watched Chauncey Billups throwing up threes like it was nothing. I even made eye contact with Rip Hamilton much to Rico's chagrin. He winked at me and Rico caught it. I had ordered another Malibu Rum and Pineapple juice and was working on my third one by half-time. I excused myself and went to the ladies room. I couldn't make it a step or two without a guy trying to holler at me. It's funny, just two weeks ago, I wouldn't have even acknowledged them but I don't know if it was the rum or some new sense of freedom I was feeling but I smiled and flirted back.

After struggling with my low rise jeans, I relieved myself and washed my hands. As I messed with my ponytail I noticed a few women looking at me. I was sure they'd seen the whole confrontation thing and were talking about me until one of the women walked up and said, "You're vest is so sharp." I smiled. thanked her and silently thanked God.

As I rounded the corner, I bumped right into Colin. You could tell this was no accident and he had actually been waiting for me.

"What's up with you Koi?" he asked me.

"What's up Colin? I'm sorry about that whole scene. If I'd known Ken was going to be here, I definitely would've passed."

"Yeah, I know it had to hurt to see you with Rico. How did ya'll hook up? You know that's Chanelle's cousin right?"

"No. I didn't. He works with me and we aren't hooked up. We're just friends. I was given some tickets and I needed someone to go with me," I explained.

"Hmm. So Nika was busy?" Colin asked.

"Colin, it's really none of your business who I brought. I don't owe you an explanation and as a matter of fact I don't owe Ken one either." I snapped back.

"So that's how you do things now. Just break up with my nigga and you dealing with a co-worker the next week? That's pretty low," he said.

"Low? I know you didn't go there. You of all people know what Ken has put me through because you were right there probably egging him on. You don't have a loyal bone in your damn body. You proved that when you tried to talk to me the first time you saw me out with Ken. So don't talk to me about low. And the by the way – Low is what your so called woman would be. You need to wise up and do the same thing I did. She ain't shit from what I hear." With that I turned my back and walked away. I stopped short of stairs and yelled, "But you can tell him thanks for the flowers." Colin was standing there with his cheeks flame red. He probably wanted to slap the hell out of me so I kept on moving.

Rico was on his cell phone when I got back to my seat. I let him finish his call and then said, "I wish we could start this night over. I'm sorry that whole thing had to happen. So do you forgive me for snapping at you?"

"We straight ma. I just wasn't feeling how he was talking to you. Plus I'm about ready to fuck Colin's ass up because they played some hoe ass game at Tonic the other night. Your boy introduced himself as Keith, and Colin went along with it."

"I don't know what that was about but let's not worry about it alright? Let's try to enjoy the rest of the game."

"I'm with that," he responded.

And that's what we did. I actually had a really good time. The Piston's won and that made it even better. As we were leaving, we linked arms so I could keep up with his long strides. The Giuseppe's were killing my baby toe, so he was practically carrying me. When we hailed a cab, he took my boot off and rubbed my feet. I was tired as hell and had drifted off. I woke up when I felt the car come to stop. Rico paid the fare and I was going to go to my car but he insisted I come up for a minute.

I welcomed the warmth of his home as he lit the fireplace and gave me a warm cup of tea. I used the cup to warm my hands. He came over and sat down with me in front of the fireplace.

We sat silently staring into the fire. Both in our own worlds. My mind was racing again. I wondered and worried about Ken and how he was doing. I wanted to comfort him but I knew I had to let it go. Rico sensed that I was battling my emotions and hugged my shoulders.

I laid my head on his shoulder. He raised my head and kissed my lips lightly. I hesitantly kissed him back. His mouth was sweet as the nectar from a peach. I slowly began to kiss him back, returning the passion I was already feeling from his kisses. He sucked my tongue and then kissed my top and bottom lip. He paid close attention to each one. I pushed my weight forward so that he would lie down and I straddled him, never missing a kiss.

I stared down at him and marveled at his good looks. He was a manly man. He kept the five o'clock shadow look and he wore it well. I kissed him again. We helped each other out of our clothes and he turned the overhead track lights out. We came back together like we belonged there. His hands explored my body as mine did his. As he lay on top of me, I welcomed the extra weight. I felt so safe. I pulled him closer to me. His tongue traced my ears and gently sucked on my lobe. He kissed my neck and sucked just enough to send a tingle to the warmest spot on my body. I felt that same tingle as the hairs on his chest rubbed against my already erect nipples. He felt me shiver and his senses guided him to my breast. I felt his penis against my leg and almost lost control. My pussy was screaming "take me" as I felt his penis throbbing as it grew to the magnificent size I had experienced just nights before. I was dripping wet and was two seconds from begging for it.

He traced my stomach with his tongue and his lips met up with my other set of lips. He parted them with his tongue in

119

search of the pearl that would send me over the edge. He was an expert at his craft and wasted no time showing me. It was only seconds later that his licking, tonguing and sucking brought me crashing into an orgasm. My body arched as I felt the currents run through my body. I pushed his head deeper and he responded by sticking his tongue in deeper. I know he felt it pulsating because he paused almost as if he wasn't sure what to do. I was in another world.

After I recovered and wanted to reciprocate the favor, he pushed me back down and said, "No, this time it's all for you."

I was surprised by his authoritative demeanor but hell, I wasn't about to question him. He came up and kissed me and I tasted my own lemony juices. I licked his lips and sucked his tongue. He leaned on his forearms to position himself to enter me. His dreads fell in my face and they smelled of cucumber and green tea. I was lost in the smell until I felt the head of his member touching the opening of my being. It was so big he had to work it in. I helped him by putting my legs on his back giving him complete access. He finally had all of it in and with each stoke I experienced nothing short of complete passion. I held onto his neck as he took me on a journey I never wanted to end. I had already cum twice and he was pacing himself so that he could bring me to what would be my third and final orgasm.

He turned me back over and laid me on my back. I waited for him to start his stroke again but he surprised me. He pushed my knees up to my face and pushed in deeper. I caught my breath because this was by no means a little brother. My body had to register what was really happening. It was that "hurt so good" type of feeling. He pushed in deeper. I screamed. Somehow he had passed the point of hurt and had touched a part of me that sent waves through my body. I found myself moving my hips and pulling his ass in deeper. I screamed as I came so hard, tears formed in my eyes. I didn't want him to move as I moved up and down on his long hard shaft. I didn't realize I was crying until he started kissing the salty tears that fell from my eyes. Rico had found my G-spot.

He Said…She Said

Chapter 17

He Said…

*O*ne, two, three… to hell with this counting shit. I don't know who said counting to ten would calm a person down. The only thing it did for me was to remind me of how mad I really was. I started walking out the Garden hoping that Koi would follow me and tell me she loved me and that we could work this out. But I never heard her voice or felt a tap on my shoulder. I felt like a damn fool. I sent her all those flowers hoping to at least put a smile on her face but that obviously didn't work because she's at the game with Rico, her new man.

When I reached the exit it was so many people walking around. Most were walking with purpose unlike me, who was going wherever the street would take me. As I walked, I thought about everything I could remember from the time I first met Koi. From the first time we'd made love to now. Now I wished I would've never met Sequoia Johnson. Who would have thought I would ever be feeling the pain I feel right now? This new person was not the woman that I knew and loved. I wouldn't have imagined in a million years that another man would be thinking of Koi as his woman and best friend. This was too much for me.

While in deep thought I felt my phone vibrating my hip and took it off to see who it was. I noticed I had several missed calls and two text messages. One of the missed calls was from Janee, another from Colin and one from Koi. Koi? I thought to myself, "Did she try to follow me? Did she try to come to my rescue before I had a nervous break down? That's my girl." That's when the dagger was pushed deeper in my chest. The 2 text were actually a long one from her. It read:

"Ken I really wish you hadn't made a scene. But that's just the way you are. It's always been all about Ken. Don't think that I don't love you but I need this

time to find out what I really want. What I thought was pure and real wasn't. I feel like our whole relationship was a lie. You took advantage of my inexperience and for this I don't think I will ever forgive you. Ken you are the only man I have ever loved and trusted but I'm not sure if you'll be the last man. I wish you the best."

I knew from that moment she hadn't come after me and wasn't even thinking about it. I took this as my cue to move on. After walking twenty blocks I got a call from Tanisha. She was yelling into the phone asking why I sold her friend out. Hell with all the confusion at the Garden I'd completely forgotten about him. I apologized and made my usual mistake of running my mouth about my problems to anyone who would listen. She was listening so intently that all I remember is flagging down a taxi and telling him to take me to the Tonic jazz bar so I could meet up with Tanisha.

Tanisha

I was flying around my room trying to get ready to meet up with Ken. Things were going just as planned. The whole scene at the Garden hadn't been planned but I would take any extra help I could get. I've invested so much of my time and money into this and it has to work. It was only a few months ago that Nika had approached me about helping her break up a bad relationship that her friend was in. I of course had no problem with that since my no good ass husband had broken my heart fucking around with any groupie that came his way. I had a vendetta against all men, so I was in.

She told me that she believed that the guy loved his woman but he wasn't right for her best friend because he kept breaking her heart. Then Nika divulged that she had even fucked him once and her friend had never found out. He supposedly blamed it on liquor but I guess Nika had fallen for him but he made it clear he was drunk and he would never leave Koi for her or anyone else. That's when she recruited me and some other chick I haven't met yet to destroy him and his relationship with her best friend Koi. I made a mental note not to trust Nika as far as I could throw her grimy ass. From what she had told me about her friend, I thought Koi sounded like a sweet girl. I thought it was a shame that she had hooked up with such a dog for a man and had a fucked up best friend at that.

That was until I walked into his office that first time. Damn I was floored. He was fine. I was used to the athletic body type and he fit right in. His suit jacket lay on his broad shoulders perfectly. When he had removed his jacket I could see the outline of his sculpted chest and abs. His arms were powerful and his firm handshake exuded confidence. Everything about him screamed "Sexy!"

He had class and style, intelligence and a body that wouldn't quit. He was a "ten" and I wanted him for my own reasons. I had promised Nika I would stick with the plan but I had my own motives. Then he had made the financial move of a lifetime and my bank account now contained more zeros than I could have ever imagined. Yeah, old boy was gonna be on my team whether he wanted to or not.

I went out to the garage to choose which car I would drive. It had to be the right one. So I chose the blue Bentley coupe that was saying, "Fuck it. I'm rich!" I threw on the new Jaheim CD I'd picked up earlier today. I arrived at Tonic in fifteen minutes. I gave the valet attendant my keys, adjusted my shirt to give them a better view of my "D" cups and went into the bar to find Ken sitting in a booth with a bottle of XO.

"Hey you. I didn't know this was a 'Bring Your Own Bottle' type of joint," I said trying to put a smile on his face. It didn't work.

"I bought the whole bottle. They charged me $250 dollars for it and it only cost $90 in the store! I'm investing my clients' money in the wrong places. I should get all you guys bars, they're making a killing."

"Ken you're too funny. So do you feel any better?"

"Naw, not at all. I really don't want to talk about it anymore either. I just want to sit here, listen to some good music, enjoy your company and get as drunk as possible, if you don't mind. I'm sorry. I'm so rude. Can I get you a drink?" he asked.

"I'll have a soda. I don't really want to drink because I have meetings all morning." I lied I just wanted to keep my head because I knew he was going to lose his.

"Okay well suit yourself." He said with the look of a drunken man.

He flagged down a waitress and told her to bring me a soda and ordered some chicken wings for the both of us. I guess this is where our story together will begin.

Chapter 18

She Said…

*T*ime was slipping away from me. It seemed like I was over Rico's house more than I was at home. I still couldn't bring myself to let him come and stay at my house. I don't know what I was waiting on. We'd basically started riding together to work but going in at separate times. I wanted to still maintain the professionalism at work.

Before I knew it three weeks had come and gone. I had dove headfirst into the GP. We had already submitted our first set of drafts to the sales team. They had come back with a few suggestions and some changes. My team was dedicated and more importantly motivated. I stayed so busy that I had little time to tend the personal chaos that was festering in the background.

Even though I was staying lots of nights at Rico's we weren't having sex every night. We both were physically and mentally exhausted from the job. It felt good to have someone next tome though. The few nights I'd stayed at home were pure torture. I heard every drip from the faucet, every creak from the loft settling. Every time the heat came on it sounded like a hurricane was flying threw the loft. My loneliness was magnified by 10. I couldn't stand it.

I had never gotten around to sending Ken his stuff and he had never called for it either. I had learned from my father by chance that he was doing well and had received several referrals from a client. I was happy for him. Though I was still angry about the chick that was in his office, I didn't wish any bad luck on him.

It was 1 o'clock in the morning and I was in my office finalizing the last drafts of the ad campaign. I had Rico going over the television spots and checking the schedules. We had finally taped the radio commercials and I had my in house techno-genius, Brett Cunningham putting the final touches to the new and improved website. We had put together a slide show presentation that would showcase everything.

Benjamin McSwain, our top sales rep, was burning a hole in my carpet pacing the floor. He had gone over his presentation a million and one times but he wanted to present it to us one more time. I felt his pain because I had been on pins and needles all day as well. I had finally released the team to their loved ones around 11 p.m. and thanked them for a job well done. The team had done all that they could do to guarantee a win on this one and I was so proud of each and every one of them. We were set to present to Mr. Reed at 8 o'clock the next morning and to the client at 10. I was exhausted.

Brett gave the thumbs up on the website and Rico signed off on the television and radio spots. We watched Ben go through the entire presentation and finally we left it in the Lord's hands.

I wanted to cry because there was some serious blood, sweat and tears put into this project, by not only myself, but my whole team. As we exited the building I shook everyone's hand and told Rico I was going home to prepare for tomorrow. I know he was surprised and maybe even a bit disappointed but I needed some time to think.

Just a month before, I would have been running home to tell Ken about my accomplishments. He would be there to encourage me and offer his support. I still couldn't bring myself to forgive him but I missed him at times like this.

When I got home I showered and wrapped my hair up. I went into his closet and pulled out his old Morehouse t-shirt that he'd had on a few nights before he left. It still smelled of his Vera Wang cologne. I pulled it over my head and it fell down past my knees. I grabbed his old ratty gray jogging pants that I had threatened to throw away so many times, and put them on.

I sat down at my computer and checked my emails. I hadn't paid a bill in 3 weeks so I needed to check my bank account and pay some bills. There were a few joint bills that we shared but I didn't have the heart to call him about some damn money. He knew that I had my own money and I didn't need the help. You would have thought he would have called though to check.

I figured he was so busy with the referrals that he'd been given that maybe he'd forgotten. This was my excuse for calling his phone at 2:30 in the morning.

My hand was shaking as I dialed the number. If I knew Ken he was probably in the bed by now. Wednesday was normally a day I could guarantee he would be at home. Especially during the play off season. The phone rang three times and I prepared myself to leave a voice mail. But nothing in a million years could have prepared me for what I heard next.

Instead of his voicemail clicking on a female voice answered his phone.

"Hello?"

I could barely get it out, "Oh. I'm..I'm sorry. I must have dialed the wrong number."

"No, Sequoia. You dialed the right number honey. Ken is sleeping right now though. I'll tell him you called in the morning." said the unfamiliar voice.

I couldn't force a word from my mouth. I closed my cell phone and sat staring at it like it was some foreign object. I replayed the call over and over mentally not sure if I was dreaming or not.

"Lord, please don't tell me another woman just answered his phone." I prayed. But who the hell was I to judge? I guess I had to face the fact the Ken had moved on as well.

He Said…

I really loved my apartment in the middle of Manhattan. I can walk to work if I felt like it. It was the kind of place I'd hoped that Koi and I would share with our kids one day. I really did miss the hell out of her, she's nothing like Tanisha. I mean Tanisha is a sweet heart but she can get on a brotha's nerves with all her "Boo this", "Baby that" and all her "I love you Ken's" and "I want to give you the world's." I mean, how can she love me when we've only been together for a couple of weeks?

I know that you can fall for someone really quick because I fell for Koi the second I'd seen her. I didn't feel that for Tanisha. We didn't have that kind of relationship, we were more like fucking buddies but she took it to another level. It's really my fault because I didn't slow her down. She was there many nights when I needed a warm body beside me but really that was it. I also think I stayed around because of her daughter Labrea. She was the coolest little girl I'd ever met. She was only six but could hold a great conversation. Whenever I wanted to leave Tanisha alone I would think about Brea and think twice about ending it.

I was laying in the bed watching her get dressed when she dropped a bomb on me.

"Ken can I ask you something?" She was looking me square in the eyes.

"Yea sure ask me anything."

"How do you feel about me?"

"Where did that come from? I mean I like you but I'm really not ready for a committed relationship right now. I really want to take things slow. The only things meant to go fast are cars and time not relationships."

"Well Ken I've got something to tell you and I don't think your going to like it." She was tapping her heel on the floor and it was starting to drive me crazy.

"Well if you knew I wouldn't like it, why did you do it?" I asked talking like I already knew what she'd done. It wasn't like I was feeling her like that so it wasn't really too much she could do to upset me.

"Last night when you were sleeping Koi called your phone. I answered it and told her you were sleep."

Except for that. Why the hell was she answering my phone? I was furious. I don't go through her purse or answer her phone. Where the hell did she get off doing some shit like that?

I was thinking frantically how to play this. If I blew up like I wanted to, she would think I still loved and wanted Koi, which I do and did. If I didn't say anything, and I decided down the line to make her my woman, she'd think she could do that anytime she wanted and I couldn't have that.

"Tanisha let me ask you something. Do I disrespect your privacy?"

"No, but..."

"Just answer the question," I said in my most stern voice.

"Then I don't expect you to do that shit to me. I don't answer your phone. Don't answer mine. That's the same shit Koi used to do and I ain't having that shit in any other relationship moving forward."

"Ken she called you at two in the morning. What the hell could she have wanted at two in the damn morning?"

"I would have known if your ass didn't pick up my phone! Besides it's none of your business what she wanted Tanisha. Again, it's my phone." I couldn't help but raise my voice a little bit.

"Ken this is ridiculous we're arguing over someone from your past. Baby, I just want to be you future."

"And you plan on getting there by showing me that you're an insecure woman before we even get past the fucking stage?"

"I can't believe you said that Ken."

"I can't believe you answered my phone Tanisha."

"I'm going home. I have to take Brea to the dentist but next time you call yourself getting mad at someone, get mad at the bitch that called you at 2 in the morning and not the one that was here in bed with you doing whatever you wanted me to do to please your ass. I love you Ken, and I know you love me so why don't you just let your guard down." Just like that she was out the door and leaving me there to soak in everything that she said.

I swung my legs over the edge of the bed and rubbed my eyes. I wasn't in the mood for this kind of bullshit. I had enough on my plate. I couldn't imagine what Koi was thinking, but should I even care?

I hadn't spoken to her since the whole blow up at the Garden. Her Dad had mentioned that she was doing really well on the shoe project she had been working on. He didn't mention us being apart so I assumed she hadn't told anyone yet. If I know Koi, she was afraid to disappoint her parents so she was keeping it on the low.

Over the past few weeks I hadn't done much other than trying to get the apartment in order. I'd neglected all my bills and all my friends. I picked up my phone to see exactly when Koi had called and I noticed a text message on my phone saying I needed to call customer service for Nextel because the bill was sixty days past due. I wondered why they hadn't cut it off yet. I called them to pay the bill and the customer service rep informed me that my contract was up. "Do you want to extend the contract on both your phones?" she asked.

"Wow," I thought to myself. This is one of the last ties that we had other than the loft. We'd maintained our own bills mainly with me paying the mortgage on the loft. If I said, "yes," I would be holding onto the possibility that we could be one again. If I said, "no," then I knew it was real, that it was really over.

I said, "Yes I would like to extend my contract but only on the main line on the account. You can shut the other one off now thanks." I already knew it was really over between Koi and I. She'd moved on and I guess so had I. DAMN…

Tanisha

That nigga has a lot of nerve, getting mad at me for answering his phone. First he acts like being with me is a damn chore and now he's fronting on me for answering his phone. I don't think I was built for this kind of abuse. I don't know why but I love him so damn much. The way he makes love to me is like no other. He takes his time with me. He's never afraid to ask "What else do I want him to do for me?" Not only what he wants me to do for him and for that I love him.

He was courteous when I introduced him to my daughter and had obviously taken a liking to her. They spent a lot of time playing that damn Play Station like it was going out of style. She'd even started asking where he was if he hadn't been around.

That's messed up because she'd never established a bond with her Dad. She knew his jersey number but not his phone number. He was too busy in the limelight to give a damn about raising his only daughter. He figured as long as the child support check was coming, she was taken care of. But that was the kind of man he was, a great television role model. Giving to all the charities, participating in the reading programs around town but had never once read a book to his own child. He'd do anything for good PR, which is why I'd received a speedy divorce and settlement. Heaven forbid he got some bad press. He hadn't even called to wish her a Merry Christmas.

I had a meeting with Nika today, so after Brea and I went to the dentist, we met Nika at the Olive Garden for lunch. As usual she was looking like a million bucks but this bitch really didn't have shit but a good mouth piece. I guess couldn't knock her hustle, she was very attractive. I'd just grown to dislike her. It seemed the more I grew to like Ken, the less I liked her.

"Hey Tanisha. Who's the little princess?"

"This is my daughter Labrea. Labrea this is Ms. Nika."

"Mommy I know who she is. She used to always kiss Uncle Sean."

The look on both of our faces was priceless.

"Uncle Sean? Baby, are you sure?"

"Yes Mommy, I'm sure. Daddy picked her up before and said that she was Auntie Nika and not to tell Auntie Pam that Uncle Sean took her on their boat. Mommy, is she really my auntie?"

The little girl really had a great memory. Nika remembered her but didn't think she would remember her.

"Yes baby, if your daddy said she's your auntie she's your auntie."

I knew this bitch wasn't shit. She'd been around my husband and never even told me. She'd probably fucked him too. Groupie Bitch. It's taking everything in me not to call Ken's ex and just come clean about this whole damn thing. She even had his best friend Colin in on this shit. I couldn't believe how this bitch was weaving this evil web of deceit and I was playing along with it. I have to put an end to this shit. But if I do that I will most definitely lose Ken and I don't think I'm ready for that.

"So, Tanisha how are things going? Is our plan still working?"

"Things are cool but I think we should probably talk about this later. We do have young ears around. You never know what might be repeated."

The way she looked at me showed me that she didn't really care who knew what. She wasn't the one that would be getting hurt she didn't fall in love with Ken. I did.

"Tanisha don't worry bout it. We can discuss this later. By the way I hope your not falling too hard. Don't get it twisted. Ken is in love with Koi and will always be. Whether they are together or not."

"Ken isn't in love with anyone except my Mommy," said Brea.

"Like I said, we should talk about this later." I said between clenched teeth. This bitch had me so pissed I was ready to slap the shit out of her.

Brea didn't miss a beat as she stayed all up in the conversation with her mom and her newfound auntie.

"Tanisha, can you excuse me? I have to use the little ladies room?"

"Sure go ahead." She got up and walked away but instead of going to the ladies room she left the restaurant and text messaged Tanisha.

"I hope you know what you're doing. I asked you to help me get back at Ken not fall in love with his ass. Get your shit together. I see how you feel about him, it's written all over your face. Get it together. Come on we are almost there. Let's finish it out."

I was pissed. It was clear she didn't just want to break them up, she wanted to destroy him and I really don't think I'm up for this anymore. I might have to just tell Ken about all of this after all.

Nika

I can't believe Tanisha's dumb ass had fallen for Ken. I thought she was the right one for the job but I should have known from the way she let her husband whore around that she was a sucker for love. I wish I could have done it myself but Ken wouldn't touch me with a ten foot pole. Besides I just wanted his ass out of the way, Koi was still my girl and I didn't want her to know that I had any parts of this.

Colin came right on in just like I thought he would. He hated being in Ken's shadow the same way I hated being in Koi's. So when I approached him at the bar and we ended up

135

back at my crib, I knew I had him. He hated Koi because he felt she had changed Ken. I scoffed at that because he was still a man-whore, what could she have possibly changed about him? But that's all I needed to put my plan in motion. By chance he mentioned that the slut bucket he was calling his woman had a cousin that had been hired in at the Reed Agency. If he was as good as she claimed he was, I knew Koi would eat him up. She took pride in her work and if she could find someone that would compliment her style and help her team; she would hire him on the spot. Then I saw him when Koi and I had gone out I almost wet my panties. He was fine! I was surprised that Koi had gone home with him that night. Not good ole' Koi. "Never cheating on my man" Koi. But the plan was falling together and that's all that mattered.

I almost felt guilty about doing this to Koi but this wasn't even about her. I was tired of being a doormat to niggas. A one night stand. Ken and I could have been good together. At least I thought we could have. When I tried to give him some he tried to act like he had some morals and shit. Well, he fucked up this time. This will teach Kenyon Burnett that this time he fucked with the wrong bitch!

Chapter 19

She Said…

*A*fter a restless night, I awoke to a cramped neck and a sore back. I'd slept all over my bed. Pillows were strewn everywhere and my white down comforter was on the floor. After hearing that chick answer Ken's phone I was fit to be tied. I'd tried everything I could possibly think of to go to sleep. I'd resorted to counting gym shoes. I dragged my ass to the shower and turned the jets on full blast. The hot water tore away at the soreness and tension. I took thirty minutes to clear my head and cleanse my mind of Ken. It was over. He had moved on in a serious way. I wouldn't even think of answering his phone even though there were countless times when I'd wanted to. She must really rank, huh?

I dressed to the nines in a St. John's suit and I pair of Mauri alligator heels. I flat ironed my hair to its full length and pin curled it to get a layered and bouncy look. I would take the curls down right before I walked out the door. I went over all my notes and mentally prepared for the meeting.

I grabbed my cell phone to call Rico and was directed to Nextel's customer service. I hung up and dialed the number again. Same results. I called my number from the house phone and was greeted by the disconnected phone message. I called the customer service line only to be informed that my phone had been disconnected this morning by the account holder, Kenyon Burnett. I couldn't believe my ears. Was it that serious? He had my phone turned off? I quickly ordered my own service and requested the same number. My service was restored almost immediately but my heart was still disconnected.

I brushed it aside and made the call that I'd originally started to make.

"Good morning Sunshine," sang Rico.

"Good morning. Did you get some rest?" I asked.

"I didn't sleep a wink. Too excited and lonely without you here. How did you sleep?"

"Fine. I was exhausted," I lied. As sweet as Rico had been the past few weeks, there was something holding me back from giving it my all.

"Well, I expect you over here tonight because we're going to have some celebrating to do," he laughed.

"Let's keep our fingers crossed. I'll see you at the office. Mr. Reed is probably already there twiddling his thumbs."

"Ok baby. I'll see you there."

I hung up feeling empty. I knew it was mainly because of the phone crap but there was something else I couldn't put my finger on. I took out the hair pins holding my curls in and my hair fell past my shoulders in layers. I combed it out and put a sheer gloss on my lips. I was ready for anything.

When I got to the office I gathered Rico and Benjamin and we met up in the large conference room. Mr. Reed soon followed. You could tell he'd had a sleepless night too. Benjamin proceeded to wow him with a five star presentation. Rico and I set back and let him do his thing. He only acknowledged us in the introduction, which was fine by me.

Mr. Reed set silent at the end of the presentation and we all awaited his reaction with bated breath. He stood up and slowly began to clap, giving us a standing ovation. We all exhaled and joined in the applause. This sealed what I'd already known. We had a winner on our hands.

Just as we expected Benjamin gave the same all star performance to the client and received the same reception. They loved it. When we returned to the office I gave the team the news and we shut down the production office and all went out to celebrate.

I took a minute to call my parents. They both knew how hard I had been working on this project. For it to come to fruition, was a dream come true. This was also the only way that

I'd been able to dodge their questions about me and Ken. As expected they both were happy for me. I promised I would come to dinner on Sunday.

The crew wanted to meet up at Fat Cat's on Christopher St. That was fine with me. I wouldn't mind a game of pool, a stiff drink and some live jazz. As soon as we got there I started a tab with the bartender. The owner of the club sanctioned of a spot in the VIP for our group and all gathered for a toast. I downed my flute of Dom and cleared my throat.

"First let me start by saying thank you. Thank you doesn't quite sum up exactly what I'd like to tell you all. You guys are the most talented people I know and I am grateful for the work that you do. You never once complained when I pushed you for more. You tolerated my "artist attitude" when I felt you weren't giving your all and pushed even harder to prove I was wrong. It's because of this commitment to your craft that we have secured one of the biggest deals in the history of the Reed Agency." They erupted into applause and cheers.

"So drink up and celebrate because you deserve it," I continued. "But you better be at work tomorrow." I laughed as they all groaned.

Rico danced his way up to me and gave me a hug. I was a little uncomfortable but I hugged him back. The hug didn't go unnoticed either. I knew the gossip lines would be open as soon as I turned my back. I whispered in his ear, "Big Brother is watching."

He replied, "Fuck Big Brother."

The night was still young as we all laughed, talked shit and shot pool. My cell phone was vibrating in my purse. I saw it was Nika. I was a little surprised because I hadn't heard much from her lately. So I excused myself to take the call. I moved down the smoky hallway that led to the restrooms.

"Hey girl. What's up with you?" I answered.

"Shit, just checking on you. Sounds like you're alright," said Nika.

"Girl, I couldn't be better. The client bought the whole ad campaign. Life is good!"

"Well damn, I guess I would be celebrating too. Where's that piece of man candy you've been hiding?" she asked.

"He's here. Girl you know he played a huge part in the whole campaign. I haven't been hiding him though. We've been immersed in the project," I answered.

"So it's official huh? You guys are a couple?" she probed.

"I wouldn't go that far Nika. We've been spending time together. I mean damn, I just got out of the relationship with Ken."

"Thank God. I don't know how you did it that long. You knew that nigga wasn't shit," spat Nika.

"Excuse me. That's enough. I don't need you to reiterate his flaws. Trust me I know all about his faults. But there is another side of Ken that you never seemed to see. He wasn't all bad Nika. He loved me. He may have had some issues but I still believe he loved me. But anyway this isn't the time or the place for this conversation. What's been up with you? Who has been keeping you company?" Koi asked.

"Same ole' same ole'. You know me. Partying, shopping, fucking and sleeping." Nika replied rather dryly.

Koi detected from her tone and attitude that Nika had a problem but she wasn't in the mood to play counselor to anyone at that moment. She had her own problems and was trying to forget about them. She moved out of the way of another patron trying to inch his way to the bathroom down the narrow hallway. He made it a point to slide as close as he could to Koi as he passed.

"Nika, well we're down at Fat Cat's if you want to come down but I have to get back to the group. We'll talk later." Koi said and ended the call.

What the hell is her problem? I haven't talked to her in days and the first thing she wants to do is dog Ken out, wondered Koi as she made her way through the crowd.

Nika

I can't believe her dumb ass. As smart as she is, she can be a damn doormat sometimes. This dummy is still sticking up for him. I don't know about her but I need Colin to tell "Dream lover" that he'd better kick it up a notch. This shit has to work.

He Said…She Said

Chapter 20

He Said…

*I*t'd been a long morning and I was hoping that the afternoon would get off to a better start. I was so pissed when Tanisha told me that Koi had called. I wanted to call her back to see what it was that she'd wanted but then I remembered I had her phone disconnected. What was I thinking?

I know that I still love Koi. I also know that Tanisha is really not the woman for me and its time for me to let her know that. As I sat there at my big old desk in my big old office, I couldn't help but wonder how all this was going to affect Labrea. I'd really grown to like her a lot. I think I'd become attached because I wanted to be a father. I wanted so badly for Koi and I to start a family. I guess I got caught up in the motions. She was the sweetest little girl and I hated that she was going to get caught in the crossfire of this whole mess. But she was Tanisha's daughter and once I made up my mind to leave Tanisha alone I would have to leave her daughter as well.

My thoughts were interrupted by the buzzing of my intercom.

"Yes Shanice, what's up?"

"Mr. Burnett, there's a gentleman in the lobby. He says that he needs to see you, though I've already informed him that you only see clients by appointment only. He still insists that he see you."

"Where did he say he was from?" I asked suspiciously.

"He wouldn't say, I asked him, he just said he wanted to see you and he will only talk to you."

"Okay well tell him to come back when he makes an appointment. I'm not in the mood for games today."

"Okay, will do."

She hung up the phone and I heard her telling him he would have to come back. Then my door flew open and in walks this huge white guy dressed in a cheap navy blue suit. He had to be at least 6'5". He seemed to be in his mid forties but as I sized him up, I figured I could still take him.

"Can I help you Sir?" I asked as I stood up behind my desk preparing for battle. Shanice had followed him in my office with a distressed look on her face. I instructed her to call security.

"Yes sir," she said as she began walking to her desk to call the boys from down stairs.

"Look Mr. Burnett that's really not called for. I just needed to deliver this to you and needed a signature," he said as he handed me a sealed envelope.

"Who is it from?"

"I'm not at liberty to tell you that but the person said you are the only person who should read this," the man instructed.

"Okay well I guess you should be leaving before security gets up here."

"Okay well just remember that this is for your eyes only."

"Yeah. No problem." As he was leaving, Shanice's ass comes back to be nosey and I told her to cancel the security and closed the door in her face as she tried to get a peek at what I was holding in my hand. But no one was more anxious to see what the envelope held than me.

Colin

"Damn girl that was the bomb. I could get used to this. You think I can get another round of that?"

"For sure. It was pretty good, huh? But you know what I love the most?"

"Naw baby why don't you tell me."

"I love sucking your dick and watching your face, it turns me on something crazy," said Nika as she sat up in the bed, letting the covers fall from her gorgeous body.

"Nika you're so damn freaky. Damn I think I love you."

"You love me? Maybe I should've been sucking you down a long time ago."

"Maybe you should have."

"I'll make a deal with you. Tell me how we're going to get back at Ken and I'll swallow all your little babies," she said as she traced Colin's stomach with her tongue.

His penis immediately started to harden at the mere mention of Nika using her oral skills again.

"Ok, Saturday we need to find a hot spot to meet up at. You bring your girl out and I'll make sure that Kim is in the place. You see they're like water and oil. Kim was heated when I talked to her last and she told me that Koi had shown up at his office," Colin explained.

"Yeah I remember Koi cried about that shit all damn night. So you'll have the Kim chick there but we need something even worse than that to get the full effect. Because I talked to her today and she really doesn't seem fazed by the situation or your little girlfriend's cousin. That's what I can't stand about her, even when I know she should be devastated she still seems calm, cool and collected."

"Don't worry baby. I'm working on it. I haven't thought that far yet, but I'll think of something just have her ass there around midnight."

"I can handle that," she said as she slipped back under the covers and sent Colin back on a wave of pure ecstasy.

He Said…

I'd just settled behind my desk to read the contents of the envelope when the same man who delivered it popped back in my office. He was singing and dancing and I realized that I'd been sent a singing telegram from Janee. After he finished his

145

number I thanked him and showed him to the door for hopefully the last time.

I opened the envelope and there was a picture of her and Lavon and a note that read:

> *Hey big brother. First let me say that I love you very much. I've been calling the house and Koi says that you aren't there. I've called when I know you're normally home but you haven't been there and you haven't been answering your cell phone. I can tell from Koi's voice that something is wrong. I know when you're ready to talk about it you will but I want you to know that I am here for and Koi both. If there is anything I can do just ask. I'll be home this weekend so let's plan on going out together. I hope my "corny white man in a suit" put a smile on your face. I almost changed it to Sponge Bob Square pants. Be glad I spared you!*
>
> *Love,*
> *J*

I love my sister but that girl is crazy. I have to make sure I call her and tell her what's going on with Koi and I. I'll have to keep it to herself because I'm not ready to tell my parents about what going on. My buzzer rang again. This afternoon was steadily going down hill.

"Yes Shanice?"

"Ms. Roberts is on the line."

"Tell her I'm in meetings and I'll call her later."

I just couldn't talk to her right now. I have a lot of thinking to do.

Chapter 21

She Said…

I should have been the happiest woman in the world but my puzzle was missing a piece. The following days after the victory celebration, I'd been flying solo. As a matter fact, I'd been avoiding Rico like the plague. The funny thing is the more I ran from him the more I felt like I was being chased.

I took a much deserved vacation from the office. I wanted to leave work, Rico, Ken and anything else related to stress behind me. I had a huge payday coming and I planned to shop my ass off. When I boarded the plane to Chicago, I laid my chair back and stretched my legs out. I ordered an apple martini from the stewardess and looked out the window as the New York skyline disappeared under a blanket of clouds. Flying first class was nothing new to Sequoia but it was something about doing it on your own dollar that excited her.

It was my plan to hit up every store on Michigan Ave then treat myself to a visit to the spa. My mom had recommended a place called Serenity Place. I was open to any suggestions at this point. I was tired of the stress. I figured after shopping till' I dropped and an hour or so of a deep tissue massage I would feel better.

It was amazing to me that I'd come to this point. Just a month ago I was in love, working hard and looking forward to my future, a future that included Kenyon Burnett. I was still reeling from the fact that he'd had my phone disconnected. I guess with a new woman in his life, those were the necessary steps to move on.

I'd decided that when I got back I was going to break things off with Rico. It was wrong from the start. Something that started off in the negative would only end up in the negative. Besides I knew better than to mix business with pleasure. Hell, he has to be one of the most talented people in the industry. I would benefit more having him on my team than having him in my bed. But make no mistake, brotha had to be one of the most talented people in the bedroom as well but that never really meant that much to me.

When Ken and I made love, it was like I was the student and he was the teacher. He introduced me to so much and it was always more intensified because I loved him so much. I don't love Rico and after the shivers and convulsions have subsided, I still don't love Rico. I need more than multiple orgasms to satisfy me.

The other thing that was stressing me was the recent attitude that I'd picked up from Nika. She seemed irritated every time we talked. Especially if I mention Ken. She's never been fond of him but now it seems like she's even harder on him since we've been apart. It's like she wants to cement the breakup, like make sure I don't go back.

That's really strange to me because even when she didn't agree with my decisions she still supported me in whatever I decided. I mean it's not like I've said that we're getting back together, as if I had a chance, seeing that he's involved now.

I ordered another apple martini and sank deeper in my bucket seat. I lifted the arm rest as there was no one in the seat next to me. I put my leg up and continued to ponder where I'd gone wrong.

I remember the first time I caught him cheating on me. He had "befriended" a little hottie who was a student at NYU. I walked in on them at a little eatery in Tribeca and he stuttered and stammered trying to explain himself. She looked on like a deer caught in the headlights. He broke it off with her right then and there, and I of course forgave him. I asked him why he'd done it and he said it was nothing, they hadn't been intimate and he would never do it again. He did. A few times and each time I forgave him. Then there was Bianca. I dealt with all the other infidelities but Bianca almost destroyed our relationship. She was the type of woman who didn't care and got joy from torturing me.

But my biggest question to him was why? I supported him in everything that he did. I let him show me how he wanted to be pleased. I was his friend and confidante. I strived to be a success because his strength and tenacity motivated me. I wanted him to be just as proud of me as my parents. That's why my success with the gym shoe campaign was bittersweet because I wanted him to be there to see me win the campaign.

My flight had arrived and my Metro Car was there to pick me up. The chauffer took me to the Grand Peninsula Hotel right in the heart of Michigan Ave. I'd actually reserved the Peninsula suite because this was the suite that Ken and I would stay in whenever we came to Chi-town. This suite was definitely five-star. It covered 3,000 square feet of the top guest floor of the hotel. There was a formal dining room with a grand piano, a private outdoor terrace with a Jacuzzi. I had spectacular views of the historic Water Tower, Lake Michigan and Chicago's Gold Coast. The master bedroom had two French doors that led out to the private terrace and also a gas fireplace. It was amazing.

I flopped down on the King-sized bed and kicked off my shoes. I couldn't help but laugh as I remembered when Ken and I made love on this same bed just months ago, in a pretty intense session of love making we'd fallen off the bed. I had bruised my behind and he ended massaging my ass instead of getting some ass. I giggled to myself as I cruised down memory lane. There was no mistaking it, I missed my man. Now what was I gonna do?

He Said…

I opened the door to the apartment a little after nine and walked into a cold space. There was a couch but no one sitting on it. There was a TV, but it wasn't on. This was a house but surely not a home. I missed everything I had with Koi and it bothered me that I had another woman ready to give me the world but I didn't want it with any one other than Koi.

I had called Tanisha before I left work and told her I would be by her place at ten. I suggested her place because, if she did decide to tell me to get out, I would be more than happy to make a break for it. But if I did this at my place, it's a good chance she might try to break something. Or even worse make me feel bad and I don't put her out and then the entire break up speech I practiced all day would be in vain.

I started gathering her things to take to her. I hadn't realized she'd accumulated so much stuff in such a short time. She had her tooth brush which was expected, but then she had stuff like house shoes, iPod and maxi pads. I mean damn, she had it all here and I hadn't even notice. That just goes to show my mind was somewhere else. I finished packing her stuff and headed out the door on a mission. I was going to set Tanisha Roberts free.

While I was in the car every sad love song came on, but never once did I think of Tanisha. I only thought of Koi and how much I missed her. I missed how every time we were in the car together I would get mad because she was always telling me how to drive. Damn I hated that but I missed it like crazy. I even missed when she tried race me in her little Benz. I could have easily beaten her but I never wanted to hurt her feelings. Besides I loved the little dance she used to do when she won.

My trip down memory lane was interrupted when I realized I'd made it to Tanisha's already. "Well here goes nothing," I said as I got out of the car and knocked on her door.

"Hey baby, why didn't you use your key?" she said looking great in her workout sweats, with her hair pulled back in a ponytail.

"I won't be needing it anymore," I said as I handed her the key which I'd never put on my ring in the first place. I guess that should've been a sign. "We need to talk."

"You came to break it off with me didn't you?" she said with a very stern look on her face.

"Yeah I did, but…"

"Ken you really don't have to explain. I understand you're not really over Koi, and to be honest I knew it all along. I just wanted to do what ever I could to make you love me like I know you love her."

Standing there in her kitchen I was at a lost for words. There was really nothing left to say, it's not like I could defend myself because it was all true. I didn't love her like I loved Koi but I didn't want to hurt her either. She was a great friend but an even better client. I wanted to save at least the business side of it.

"Tanisha, you're right, I do love Koi and it's not fair to you and Brea. My heart is with Koi and I really don't think it ever left."

"You're a really good man and I don't doubt that you could be the man for me if your heart was in it. I'm not sure what type of man you were to Koi but obviously she must have been a hell of a woman to you. But I wanted to tell you something."

"What is it?"

"Don't think for one minute that I don't love you and want to be with you. I guess the timing was just off a little."

"Yeah it was but I have to say you are handling this much better than I thought you would."

"I've been preparing for this since Koi called. I saw your face when I told you that she had called. You wear your heart on your sleeve. I figured she must've come to her senses."

"I haven't even talked to her yet but I plan on calling tonight. I just hope it's not too late."

"I hope so too. You deserve to be happy. I'm praying for you. But if you change your mind I'll be here waiting."

I reached out to give her a hug but she turned her back to me and walked out of the room. As I turned to leave I saw Labrea standing there with tears in her eyes. I couldn't take it any longer and just walked out.

I didn't think it would be that hard. I knew I had developed some feelings for her but it wasn't love. I didn't want to hurt her anymore than I already had and I knew this was the best thing.

I got back home and called Nextel and got the automated service so I logged on to the computer to reconnect Koi's phone and I noticed she was logged in on her Yahoo account. I took a chance and instant messaged her:

Hey you. How are you? Can we please talk? I have so much I need to say to you.

Now as I sit here waiting for her to respond, I hope I did the right thing.

Tanisha

I sat on my bed and tried to regain my composure. I knew this was coming. I had no business messing with him in the first place. Listening to that stupid tramp Nika. I was fine by my damn self spending my time and money on my daughter. I had to ask myself though, "What do I do to make men leave me? I'm a good woman. What am I doing wrong?"

"I'm through with men," I declared. "I can't blame Ken for this though. I blame that bitch Nika. What am I saying? I should be blaming myself. I should have never helped that bitch try to break them up. I knew better, what was I thinking? I know she's going to really be upset when I tell her he dumped my ass. I swear I started to tell Ken about this whole damn scheme. Maybe it wouldn't have made him stay with me but I would at least have a clear conscious. So she better be happy that I didn't do that."

I started to call her ass to let her know what had happened but decided against it. I ran me some bathwater and tucked my baby in, who had yet to ask what had happened but I knew she already knew. She hugged my neck tight and told me it was going to be alright. She was the only person who loved me unconditionally and at that moment my love for her grew even more. I vowed that from this point forward I would lead by example.

I settled into my bath and heard my cell phone buzzing. I looked at the screen and it was Nika. It was like she had a radar for when things went sour in her plan. Whatever the case, she would have to wait until tomorrow. I had some thinking to do.

He Said…She Said

Chapter 22

She Said…

9 was exhausted from walking all up and down Michigan Avenue. I'd spent so much damn money that most of the stores agreed to just send my packages over to my hotel. I had just plugged in my laptop and got down into the Jacuzzi tub when I had an instant message pop up on the screen.

When I saw it was from Ken I almost lost my laptop! I read it again:

Hey you. How are you? Can we please talk? I have so much I need to say to you.

At first I was elated, because I had so much to say to him as well. But then I thought about the woman that answered his phone and the fact that he had turned my phone off and immediately those feeling were traded in for feelings of anger.

My cell phone was ringing so I checked the screen, it was Rico. I exhaled because I really wasn't ready to field any questions from anyone, especially not him. I answered anyway.

"This is Sequoia."

"Hey baby. I was just checking to see how your trip was going and to see if you needed any company."

"I'm fine, actually having a ball. How are things at the office," I asked ignoring his last question.

"Everyone is still pretty pumped up. We had a few more projects come in but I really think this is the calm before the storm because word in the streets is that everyone has heard about the GS project and are looking to shoot a ton of business our way. But I miss my boss."

"Well it sounds like things are running ok without me. I'll only be a few more days and I think we should talk when I get back," I said.

155

"Why, is something wrong?"

I knew he suspected that I was going to break things off. I'd honestly been trying to be as distant as possible. It was something about starting and trying to maintain something that was never supposed to be. I know that my heart is elsewhere and to try to have something with some else was unfair to the person and even more to myself.

"Yes, something is wrong. But we'll talk about it when I get back."

I hung up and pondered if I should respond to Ken or not. My mind was telling me no but my heart was telling me yes.

My heart won:

I need to talk you too. I'm in Chicago now. I'll call you when I get back.

I planned on enjoying the rest of my trip. Stress free. Tomorrow was my spa day and I was going to kick it with a true friend, Chyna Stewart.

He Said…

So she answered me, but it's really a bittersweet victory. She did say she was out of town and she'd call me when she got back. But what was so important that we couldn't talk tonight? Right now? Or for that matter if she wanted to talk to me too why hadn't she called me before she left? Why did we have to talk when she returned from her trip? All these questions were running through my head. I really wanted to know what she wants to talk about. Does she really just want to end it? Is it official? Are she and Rico going to be an item? The new power couple at her job?

I was driving myself crazy. Sitting here with nothing on my mind but her. I can't handle this. I need to go out and have a good time but I'm not sure where I should go. I do know that I don't want to run into Tanisha or anyone that she knows. I guess I don't have to worry about Rico because he's out of town banging the shit out of Koi. Or at least I assume that's where he is, that's where I would be if she would let me. Man, I'm going crazy! I've got to get out of here. I called Colin to see what he was up to.

"Hello?" he answered.

"What's good Ken?"

"Nothing. I'm about to go down the street to ESPN Zone and grab a chicken salad and a beer. Why don't you meet me there?"

"Cool I'm with that. I need to go out for a minute, plus I'm sure they have some of the college games on. I need to check these kids out so I can know who is who when the draft comes out."

"Ok. Well I'll see you in about a half."

"Cool, a half it is. One."

Colin

I hung up and had to formulate my plan. "Okay think Colin. Think. How am I supposed to get Ken to agree to coming out on Saturday? Ever since that incident at the Gardens, he's been on that all work and no play tip. That shit took a lot out of him. I saw it all on his face. He was beat and I loved it. He's played me like a fool so many times. He cheated with my girl and thought I didn't know but I did. He even had the nerve to act like he didn't know what was up with Mark and Chanelle. When all along he was the one fucking her, and I'm sure he had something to do with Mark getting a piece. So helping Nika get back at him wasn't for her sake it was all mine. My first thought was an eye for an eye, but Koi wouldn't think about fucking with me so whatever I have to do, I need to make sure this nigga feels the pain."

I quickly dressed in my normal gear, a Piston Jersey with a black tee under it, with some crispy Rocawear Jeans and some wheat color Timbs. I hopped on the train to meet this nigga who calls himself my friend. I can't wait to pull the knife out of my own back and use it on my "friend."

When I arrived at ESPN Zone, Ken was looking like the sorry bastard that I know he is. I put on my game face.

"Ken what's good man?"

"Nothing much man. Just thinking about the message I got from Koi today."

"Really? I didn't know ya'll was talking again," I said.

"I wouldn't say we're talking. It was more like I instant messaged her and she agreed that we should talk when she got back. That shows a little glimmer of hope. At least I know she isn't so mad that she won't talk to me. We might still have a chance," Ken said.

"That's cool, I guess. I mean how do you feel knowing another man has been tapping that? I mean, it's easy to say you want her back but when, or should I say if you get her back can you forget about that or will it always be in the back of your mind?"

"I really don't know. I'm just trying to see where her head is. She might not even want me back. Knowing what a businesswoman she is, she might just want to clear up all our loose ends and go our separate ways. Have you talked to Rico or Chanelle? Do you know where they stand?"

Sitting here listening to him made me hate him even more. He was making himself sound so innocent. He had the nerve to fuck my girl and then sit here like he's never done anything to deserve what Koi is dishing out. This fool shouldn't be in the financing field, he should be a damn actor! He's got Denzel beat.

"I don't know. Man, I think since Rico knows you're my best friend, he ain't trying to tell me shit. I really haven't been kicking it with Chanelle either."

"Yeah, I guess you're right. I broke it off with Tanisha today."

"What! Get the hell out, you did?" The grin on my face was only to make him think I was still on his side.

"Yeah man I had to put that relationship to bed. I couldn't keep playing with that woman's heart. She's a great girl. She would have been a good woman but my heart is somewhere else."

"I feel that, well maybe it is for the best. How did the little girl handle it?"

"That was the crazy thing. I turned around to leave and she was standing there with tears in her eyes. That shit was too much for me. I saw the hurt of a thousand women in that little girl's face."

"Damn Ken. I didn't know you cared that much."

"That's the thing. I'm changing, man. I just hope it's not too late. I don't think I can make it without Koi. I'm done hoeing around. That's my future."

"I feel you. Yo, order me another beer man. I have to drain the snake."

"Okay I got you."

As I made my way to the restroom I had to calm myself down. I was two seconds from making a mad dash. I had to tell Nika to get on her girl because the plan was going down the drain fast. All of a sudden the plan that we thought was so well planned was going from sugar to shit!

She answered on the first ring like she was expecting my call.

"Hey baby. I thought you were going to meet Ken. What happened?" she asked

"I did. I mean, I am. I'm still here and I can't talk long. I wanted to tell you that he broke up with your girl today."

"Get the hell out of here!" the change of tone in her voice showed me that if I didn't have her attention before, I definitely had it now.

"Yup, he just told me and to make shit even worse he's been talking to Koi," I told her.

Nika almost dropped the phone. "What! Baby let me go. I've got some shit I have to fix."

"Alright, I'll see you later on tonight."

"Not tonight. I have to fix this shit. I'll see you for breakfast in the morning."

She was mad as hell! I couldn't blame her, this shit had to work. When I got back to the table Ken was talking to some white guys with suits on. I used that as my in to get up out of there. I really didn't want to be in that snobby ass conversation plus I got what I needed from him already tonight.

Chapter 23

She Said…

9 woke up bright and early and took a cab to Serenity Place Day Spa. My girl Chyna Stewart had a real deal money maker on her hands. It was 9:30 and the place was already pumping. I was met with hugs and kisses from Chyna and the staff. We went into her office to talk before I started my treatments.

"What's going on girlfriend?" I asked as I sat down in her seating area.

"Girl, nothing much. Business as usual. You know how I do it," Chyna replied. "What's been up with you? I hate to say it but you look a little tired. Don't tell me I'm gonna have to ride to the NYC and kick Ken's behind."

"Girl, that's just part of my problem. I just completed a really big ad campaign and they bought it so that's why I'm down here to treat myself, by myself. Now Ken, that's a whole 'nother story. You might not have enough time for me to run that down," said Sequoia.

"Please. You are my girl. I'll make time for you," said Chyna as she slid down next to Koi. She called Gabrielle in to bring them some iced-tea and Koi began her story.

"Well, things have been shaky between us ever since I found out about that Bianca chick when he and Colin came here that time. I've just been unable to trust him. Then with me constantly working, I think that just gives him the time to do whatever. But what am I supposed to do? I've worked hard to get where I am in the business and I'll be damned if I stop just so that I can babysit my man. I remember a time when how I felt mattered to him. Then I come into his office a few weeks ago and there's this tramp there basically telling me that she's been fucking him for months and she knows all about me. That was just the straw that broke the camel's back. But to add to the drama, I had my own little affair and I've been seeing the guy ever since. The worse part about that is he's a coworker." She paused, waiting for Chyna's response.

"What? I can't say anything about that. My fiancé is a co-worker. It's nothing wrong with that, in my opinion. What I'm more surprised at is the fact that you cheated," she said. "That's not like you at all."

"I know. It kind of just happened. We'd been working really closely on this project and he is sexy as all get out. I was mad at Ken because he'd done another disappearing act, me and Nika went out and Rico was there and so went the story," said Koi as she exhaled and put her head in her hands.

"Nika? Hmm I knew she wasn't far removed from the story. I know that's your girl, but she is a shady character," said Chyna. "It's just something about her that rubs me wrong. I wouldn't trust her around my man."

"It's funny that you would say that because lately every chance she gets she is bad mouthing Ken. I mean, she's always been protective of me but just recently it's been a little over the top," replied Koi.

"Yeah, I would definitely keep my eye on her ass. I wouldn't be surprised if she was trying to get up on him," said Chyna, trying to put a bug in Koi's ear.

When Sequoia and Nika had come to Chicago for the Taste fest and a few hair shows it was so obvious to Chyna that Nika was extremely jealous of Sequoia. Koi was a pretty woman on top of a having the perfect personality. She commanded attention when she walked in the place and held it because of her bright personality. Chyna was the same way but Nika's gold digger attitude shown straight through her fake exterior. Now, she was a beautiful woman, but Chyna could see through all the bullshit. And she always had reservations about Koi having her around Ken. He was what Nika wanted. A fine ass successful man with money and Nika was the kind of chick that would cross that line if you let her. Unfortunately, Chyna also knew that Ken was the type to fall for the temptation as well. She just prayed for the sake of her friend that the vibe she was feeling was wrong.

"So tell me about this Rico character," asked Chyna.

"A character he is. It's like he came from nowhere and turned my life inside out. He's gorgeous Chyna," emphasized Koi. "He's everything that any woman would want in a lover. He's intelligent and talented…"

"And??" said Chyna.

"But he isn't Ken," said Koi with tears in her eyes. "I love him Chyna. I really, really miss him. I miss everything about him. I want to see him sitting on the couch when I get in late from work, mad at me but still there. I want to hear him snoring next to me in bed. I wanted him to share my happiness and to be proud of me when I sold the campaign. I miss him so bad it hurts. Rico is everything that any other woman would want but I don't. I want my soul mate. But the other thing is, I called Ken's phone the other day and a woman answered the phone. So he's seeing someone else and it must be serious because he wouldn't ever let a woman answer his phone." said Koi.

"I don't know about that though Koi. He may be seeing someone but he's obviously still thinking of you if he sent you that message this morning. But you don't need a pep talk from me, Koi. You already know what you want and who you want. So do what you have to do. Get your man back. As far as Rico is concerned, he knew what he was getting into when he met you. And usually if it seems too good to be true, it usually is. He'll understand; if he doesn't, screw him. But don't forget what I said about Nika. You have to keep your eyes wide open. Don't ignore the obvious," warned Chyna. "Ok, you are in need of a serious massage. Let's go get you started and we'll hook up later for dinner," she said as she hugged Koi and rubbed her back.

"Thanks Chyna for lending me your shoulder," said Koi wiping her eyes.

"Don't worry. I'll put the cost for my consultation in your bill. You can afford it, big money!!" joked Chyna.

As she sat in the sauna Koi thought about the things that Chyna had warned her against. She leaned her head back on the wall and said to herself, "You're right Chyna. I'll be watching."

Chapter 24

He Said…

*L*ast night after I left ESPN Zone, I stayed up half the night wondering what was going through Koi's mind. I felt like an ass after disconnecting her phone. Now I want to talk to her and I'm sure she has had her service restored but is it the same number? Another thing that was bothering me was I couldn't understand why Colin left so abruptly after our conversation. I don't remember talking about his girl because I know they are on the outs. We only talked about my situation. I did ask him about Rico and Koi, so maybe that would have made him uncomfortable, but damn, did he have to leave? But he's been acting real funny lately anyway. I know that girl has him sprung but he's never been tripping like this. I'll have to pick his brain later today. But right now I had to get my work out on and get a bite to eat because I had to pick Janee up from the airport. Her flight was coming in at nine so I had time.

"I am so sick of love songs," blared from my speakers when I started the car. I cut the radio off so fast I damn near broke the knob. I love the song but it hit too close to home right now.

It was a pretty gloomy day and as I raced to LaGuardia I wished that I'd worn a heavier jacket. I knew that I was going to have to park and go look for Janee because it would be easier than circling around, waiting for her. I still had a few minutes before her flight landed so I perused through the magazines at the little gift shop. As I glanced up I saw a face from the past that I wished I would never see again. It was the chick Bianca who I'd fucked with in Chicago. What was she doing here?

I acted like I didn't see her and just kept it moving. She was the one person I couldn't be caught dead with because if Koi ever saw her it would be World War III in New York City. I really don't know how it went down but from Koi's version of the story Bianca had told her all about our little fling and told her that if she was taking care of me then I wouldn't be calling her for booty calls. Though I'd actually never hit, I was working on it, but all this went down before I got a chance. Bianca said Koi called her so she told her what she wanted to hear. I cut her dumb ass off right then because she already knew I had a woman and any other hoe on the side knows that no matter what you never talk to the main woman! Like I said, I don't know how it went down but she is the last person that I want to see right now.

Fortunately Janee's plane arrived on schedule. I met her down at the baggage claim and was surprised to see my little sister looking like a very grown woman. It was amazing what a few months of college could do to a girl. She had her hair down and her make-up on. I noticed the men taking second glances and hurried my butt over to where she was standing. She gave me a hug and told me to get her bags. That's one thing that hadn't changed. She was still ordering me around even though I'm the oldest.

Once we made it back to the truck she surprised me by saying, "I'm really disappointed in you how you played Koi."

"Come on Janee. Man, I know I've done some dirt but I've changed since then. That was some old shit that came back to haunt me. But she ain't so innocent. You know she's fucking around with some dude now."

"Boy please! You been cheating forever. I can't believe you're trying to act like the victim here. Koi loved you and you played her, Ken. Did you ever think your bullshit might have pushed her right into his arms? Get over it Ken. Mama didn't raise a coward, she raised a man. Take responsibility for the pain you caused that girl. You never knew how much we used to talk and still do. Koi is my girl and I knew about everything that was going on. She didn't tell me about Rico until after you moved out because she didn't want to put me in the middle of it."

"So you know we're not living together right now?"

"Yes I knew. I called her when I couldn't get in touch with you and she told me then what was going on. Ken I'm sorry, but you kind of deserve some of this."

"Yea, your right, I do. It's time for me to get my shit together because Janee I really do love her. I love her so damn much and I want my girl back. Do you think I have a chance?"

"I really don't know. You're going to have to talk to her about that. I do know she's coming home today. She went to Chicago alone to shop and see her friend. Why don't you just call her later today?"

"I would but she said she would call me so I'll just sit and wait. But Janee thanks, I needed that. But I want you to know that I really do want her back."

"Well act like it dummy! And if you do get her back, you better treat her like you would want someone to treat your daughter or me and it'll all work out."

I pulled the truck in front of my parent's house and popped the trunk. Janee had already made her way up to the front door.

"No don't worry about your bags. I'll get them," I joked.

She flipped me the bird and went on in the door. One thing I was happy about was the fact that now I knew that Koi had gone to Chicago alone and not with Rico. That was another thing giving me sleepless nights. I grabbed the luggage and trudged up to my parents' door.

She Said…

After my spa treatment I felt like a new woman. My body felt wonderful and after my free therapy session with Chyna, I was in a better state of mind as well. I had a plan and I was going to stick to it. When I got back to my room, I sat down and put my thoughts on paper. The first thing that I was going to take care of was breaking up with Rico. That was all wrong from the start.

167

And it isn't fair for me to have him dangling along while things are still up in the air with me and Ken. What we did was a mistake and I'm willing to admit that and I planned to fix it. Secondly I was going to keep a better watch on the people closest to me. I had noticed a change in Nika's attitude and if Chyna had picked up on something as well, then it was worth looking into. I hated to have to think this way because I really thought Nika was my best friend. But I figured I could never be too safe.

The next thing I did was write down a list of pros and cons to my relationship with Ken. I figured I'd get all the negatives out of the way first. The cons to our relationship are:

1. *He's a cheater*
2. *He has lied to me*
3. *He doesn't respect my job*
4. *He divulged personal info about me to another woman.*

I couldn't think of any more but that was more than enough. Just reading the list made me sick. So I started on the pros. The pros to our relationship are:

1. *He is my soul mate*
2. *He makes me laugh and smile*
3. *He is a God-fearing man*
4. *He is successful and intelligent*
5. *My parents love him*
6. *He'd do anything in the world for me*
7. *He is tolerant of my crazy ways*
8. *I love his family*
9. *I can see us growing old together*
10. *He loves me like no other man has ever loved me before*

I couldn't stop crying as I wrote line after line. I know my man loves me. He loves me enough to change. I threw myself into my career when things got bad for us. I never stopped to think that maybe I needed to try to make it work too. I'm not perfect and I've proved that by dealing with Rico. But if we both committed to making this work it could happen. My man can change. The question is does he want to?

I decided to have my packages sent home from the hotel. Trying to transport all this crap in the airport was going to be impossible. I kept the gifts that I'd bought my parents, Nika and Janee out and sent everything else with the hotel employee they'd sent to retrieve my things. As I waited for Metro Car to send a limo to get me, I went into the very high end gift shop in the lobby. It looked more like a store on Fifth Ave in New York. I saw a pair of stunning platinum cufflinks in the case. They were beautiful. I asked to see them and weren't surprised to see they were $1100. I gave the sales lady my Black Card and had her wrap them for me. I had the perfect businessman in mind to give these perfect cuff links to.

Finally my car arrived and I laid my head back and thought about exactly what I was going to say.

He Said…She Said

Chapter 25

He Said…

"*Hey Colin. It's Ken. You're going to be really upset with me but I can't make it. I hate to leave this on your machine but my mom is going through one of her things, thinking about my brother and I really think I need to just chill with her tonight. Look man I tried to call your cell phone and I just got your answering service so I hope I caught you in time. I called the manager at the Pure club and got you guys Jay's Room for the night and everything is on me. Get whatever man. I'll talk to you later. One.*"

I was hoping the guys would understand because my Mom's well-being was more important to me. I haven't really talked to my mom in a while because I was trying to avoid answering any questions about Koi. Ever so often she goes through a spell. I can't imagine what it's like to lose a child but I know what I felt like losing my brother so I know what she is going through is probably magnified 10 times.

I remember when Lavon first died my mom really was really broken up and what made it even worse is my dad just threw himself into his work as his way of dealing with it. I don't understood how they managed to stay together. Their whole relationship changed when Lavon died. I've long since been gone and with Janee living in Atlanta now I worry about them a lot.

I arrived at my parent's house a little before ten and started to knock on the door when I remembered I had a key to my childhood home. It was a beautiful place indeed. As a child I never realize just how fortunate we were. I honestly thought all of my friend's houses were just as big and nice as ours. I remember going to visit a cousin who lived in an apartment and he and his friend were teasing me, calling me a spoiled little rich kid. It was surprising to me because our parents raised us to be humble. My brother and I ended up beating the guy up because we may have been rich but we weren't anybody's punk. I laughed to myself.

I walked in and was greeted by the smell of some serious soul food being cooked. I looked at my watch to be sure of the time. I couldn't believe Ms. Wells, the cook would be up this late cooking. She had been with our family for as long as I could remember. I walked into the family room and noticed my mom in her robe looking at one of our family photo albums. I could see the tears in her eyes. My dad was out of town on business and this just clarified that it was best that I canceled my plans with the fellas tonight. My Mom didn't need to be alone.

"Hey Mom, what's going on?" I asked trying to break the ice. I sat on the chaise lounge beside her like I used to when I was seven years old.

"I was looking at this picture of your father and Janee. It's amazing how fast that child has grown. I wanted to thank you for talking me into allowing her to go to Spelman. I was afraid to let her go but I think the independence has really helped her. Did you see her today? She looks like a grown woman."

"Yea Mom, I was thinking the same thing. I almost had to beat some old man up with his cane for looking at my sister like he wanted her."

There it was. That made her smile. I had finally broken the ice.

"Ken you can't protect her forever. I actually learned that from you," she said as she wiped her eyes and stretched her arms.

"Yes I can. I just bought a new gun."

"Boy, shut up and give me a kiss."

I leaned over and kissed her cheek and we continued to peruse through the albums together. There were years and years of pictures of my entire family. I'd seen them all a million times before but the picture that caught my attention was the one of

Koi and I in my parents' pool. I remember it was from last summer. Right before Koi and I started having our problems.

I closed the album and stood up to stretch my legs. "Mom, where's Janee?"

"Sequoia came and got her right after you left. They went out for bite to eat, I think. Why you didn't tell me you guys were having problems?"

"Because Ma, I think I was kind of ashamed of how I handled the entire situation. I really messed things up with her and I really want her back. I catch myself thinking about her all night, all day. Mom I can't eat. I really hate what's going on," I explained.

She rubbed my back and sat back down. "Well what are you going to do Ken? Are you going to let her get away? Tell Koi how you feel. Boy, I do want some grand babies before I get too old to chase after them."

"I'm gonna do whatever I have to do."

We heard the front door close and Koi and Janee walked in talking not even noticing Mom and I standing there. I watched her face for a reaction. I saw surprise first then to my surprise I saw relief.

Colin

"He did it again. He sold me out right when I planned this night to a tee. His damn Momma calls and his ass goes running right over there. Damn Momma's Boy. This is a damn disaster. Nika's gonna be pissed that he called it off. Nika had Koi coming. Everything was set to go down today. Fuck it. I'm gonna go to the club and chill anyway."

My cell phone rang. I checked the screen it was Nika. "Damn!"

"Yeah?" I answered.

"Hello?"

"Hey baby. I have some bad news."

"What you mean you have some bad news? Tonight is the night, what's going on?"

"Well Ken sold us out at the last minute. I did everything in my power to get him to come but he wasn't having it. He didn't want any parts of coming out tonight. Something is going down with his Mom."

"Come on Colin. I'm on my way and I got Koi coming. I had to go through hell trying to get her to come out tonight. She was already complaining because she just came in from her trip and was tired but I managed to get her to come out. So you have to do something."

"Look baby I tried, he's not coming," I explained.

She switched her tone really quick, "Damn. Do I have to do everything? Just get him here. I don't care how you do it. Just do it."

"It's not that simple Nika. You need to try to understand when Ken makes up his mind there's no changing it."

"Damn that nigga got all of you thinking he's the king or something. You can at least try."

"You know what? Hold on. You think you know every damn thing. You need to hear it for your self." I clicked over on my phone and dialed Kens cell and joined Nika in, he answered almost immediately.

"Hello, what's up Colin?"

"Yo, you need to meet me at the club man. We can't have a good time if you don't come out and kick it with us."

"I talking to Mom about a few things and Koi and my sister just walked in so I really have to let you go. Go on and enjoy yourself. I'll kick it with you tomorrow." He hung up the phone.

"Like I said he doesn't budge when it comes to his family. And what is your girl doing over there if she's going out with you?"

174

"We were supposed to hook up in about an hour. Let me go so I can see what's going on. Damn this is getting on my nerves!" she hung up without saying goodbye

She was starting to get on my damn nerves. I was really starting to question what her motivation behind all this was. Couldn't nobody be working this hard at getting back at her friend's boyfriend just for her friend's sake. I definitely wasn't feeling the way she had been talking to me lately. I was really feeling like she was using me.

I really don't know what Nika's going to do now that it seems like her plan is falling off. I needed to talk to Tanisha to see what happened with her and Ken. I was surprised to here that Koi was over his Mom's. What is that all about? Well I ain't worrying about it tonight. I got ready to roll out to meet the guys at the bar. I guess I should have been pissed but tonight it was on Ken. I'm going to let Nika worry about Ken and her home girl.

She Said…

To say I was shocked to see Ken standing there would be the understatement of the century. Janee told me that he had picked her up from the airport and stayed over for a while earlier so I definitely didn't expect to see him here tonight. I know his Mom was having a tough time with his brother's death. It had been years, but who can put a time on mourning? Especially your child. One of the most intimate moments that he and I had shared was when he told the story of how his parents had come to his school to tell him that his brother had been killed in an accident. My heart bled for him as I recalled how torn up he was. His mother told me that he had never really talked to anyone about it. I felt honored but it hurt me to see him so hurt. It was the only time that I'd ever seen him cry. But right now I just hoped to God that the surprise that I felt hadn't registered on my face but I

175

knew it had because that was something that Ken always told me, that I wear my emotions on my sleeve.

His mother broke the awkward silence and I was so grateful. "So you ladies finally made it back. I had actually whipped up some black-eyed peas and rice."

Ken shifted where he was standing. "I thought Ms. Wells was cooking. So you can still burn, huh old lady?"

"Boy please, I could teach Ms. Wells a thing or two," she answered slapping him in the head.

We all laughed. Janee called herself being slick. I saw her open her cell phone like it had rang and faked a conversation as she walked out of the room to hang her jacket up. Mrs. Burnett gathered her mug from the table and asked if I wanted any tea and made her exit to the kitchen.

There we were looking stupid as hell. He looked good as usual. I on the other hand was dressed way down in a Juicy jogging suit and gym shoes. My hair was pulled back with not a glimmer of lip gloss. I broke the silence this time. I hadn't rehearsed for hours and hours for nothing.

"I love you," I said. He started to respond but I stopped him. "You have dogged me out. Disrespected our relationship and put our business in the street. I tried my hardest to be everything that I thought you wanted but maybe I didn't try hard enough or maybe I wasn't sure exactly what it was you wanted me to be. But I can only be me. Sequoia Nicole Johnson. I won't change the person I am for anyone ever again. I'm capable of loving and trusting you unconditionally but only if you can do the same for me. I forgive you for the things that you have done and I hope that you can forgive me for the things that I have done. I have searched my soul for a reason to hate you but I serve a forgiving God and if he can forgive us for all the sins we've committed then I damn sure can forgive you. I don't know if there is a chance for us but I know that you are my soul mate and I love you with all my heart. We belong together. We climbed the ladder of success together. You encouraged me and I motivated you. We are supposed to grow old together. I see that you have moved on and I've never been one to try to court someone else's man but I want my man back."

I paused to catch my breath and he walked up to me. I was so scared I was shaking. But I kept my stance. I hadn't been this close to Kenyon in over three months. I smelled his Unforgivable cologne and melted in my shoes. He wrapped his arms around me hugged me so tightly. I felt his tears falling onto my forehead. He was crying! I couldn't believe it. This wasn't the reaction that I was expecting. I expected him to start lying his way out of this. Or maybe I expected him to say "Screw you. You've been dealing with that other guy. I don't want you." I don't know what I expected but this was not it.

I held him for 5 full minutes before he pulled back and kissed me. There was a huge difference in what I was feeling at the moment than what I had felt when I was in Rico's arms. I felt like I belonged here. We fit like a glove. I wiped his tears away and we kissed again and then he started to speak.

He Said...

"I really don't know where to start. I've hurt you so many times and I know sorry won't work this time. As it shouldn't, I should have never had to tell you that again. I've been up a lot of nights wondering what you've been doing. I can't tell you how mad it made me imagining another man touching you but I have to be man enough to admit that I probably deserved it. I haven't treated you like the woman I love, the woman that I want to have my children, the woman I want to grow old with. Koi, I really don't know what you want me to do – you call it and it's done. I'm ready to be what you need me to be. Because you are all I need, you are part of me and without you I am so incomplete."

177

I couldn't contain myself anymore. The tears were flowing in streams by then. Sequoia comforted me. "Ken baby, stop crying. You're going to make me cry."

"I'm crying because I love you so much. I didn't realize how much until I didn't have you anymore. You mean the world to me Sequoia. Your Dad helped me out a lot because he kept reminding me that we belong together and that he believed that you still loved me. I think that's the only thing that let me sleep at night."

Sequoia pulled back from my embrace. "Why didn't you call? Then you had my phone turned off. I was pissed."

"I did call. I even came to your office, but the damn gatekeeper at your office kept telling me that you weren't in or you were in a meeting. She wasn't budging. Shit, I want her to come work for me."

We both let out a light laugh.

"But on a serious note, baby, I love you so much. The disconnecting the phone thing was just me being silly. I didn't know what else to do to get back at you. I realized how dumb that was when I couldn't get in touch with you. Hey, I even sent you flowers."

Koi laughed, "No Ken. You sent me the entire flower shop. You know you be overdoing it."

"No, that's not true. I was just trying to give you what I thought you deserved. Baby, I want to come home. I want to treat you like you deserve to be treated. I promise to love you and take care of you."

"What about your new chick?" Sequoia asked.

"We weren't that serious and when I explained to her that we couldn't be together because you are the only woman I want and she understood that. What are you going to do about your little boyfriend? I don't think I can handle you two working together."

"Well I can't just fire him Ken. I'll have to see how all this works out. There is a protocol that I have to follow in regards to that work situation," said Koi as she scratched her head, deep in thought.

"You know that he's Colin's ex-girlfriend Chanelle's cousin?"

"No I didn't but that explains why Colin was up at my job a few weeks ago."

"What? That's strange why did he say he was there?"

"I didn't even ask him. He didn't even know I saw him. You know I don't have any words for that nigga."

I thought that was kind of strange. I couldn't understand why Colin would go up to Koi's job without letting me know he was going. I made a mental note to ask him. My guess is that he was up there to check Rico. I know Colin. If he thought for one minute that someone was trying to do something to hurt me he would have a fit. It would be hell to pay to who ever crossed me in front of Colin." I said.

"Well it didn't look like he was confronting him. But I guess it had to be for a good reason," Sequoia dismissed it. "Well, let's start out slowly Ken. There are problems in our relationship that need to be discussed further. But as long as I know that you are committed to making this work, so am I."

"Baby, I'm giving you my heart and everything that comes with it. My job is to make you the happiest woman in the world."

She let me pull her back in and gave me the longest, most passionate kiss I think I've ever had until we were interrupted by her cell phone ringing.

"Who is that?" I asked a slight bit irritated.

"It's Rico," she said. "Damn what am I going to do?"

We both looked at each other and she kissed me and pressed talk.

He Said…She Said

Chapter 26

Rico

I don't know what's been up with Sequoia lately. I knew when I first saw her that I was going to fall in love with her. I should have never listened to Chanelle and her stupid ass man. I couldn't have been happier when Mr. Reed approached me with that job offer. I should have kept it strictly business but no, I had to mention to Chanelle who I was working with and her big mouth ass mentioned it to Colin and all of a sudden I'm in the middle of some huge conspiracy to break Koi up with her man.

I owed Chanelle a favor because she let me stay at her house when my old lady threw me out and I figured what the hell, Sequoia is fine as hell and I wouldn't mind hitting that. But then I started developing feelings and then I had my own personal agenda. I could break them up and Chanelle and Colin would be happy and then actually stay in the relationship with her because I truly think I love her.

Now ever since we sold the Gym Shoe Deal she has been acting so distant. I knew in the beginning that it would be tough because she has mad love for her nigga but I thought I had broke down that barrier she had placed up. We had been spending a lot of time together and now I can barely catch her. When she told me that she was going to Chicago, alone, I was hurt. I've got to find out where we stand because I'm starting to feel like her ex-boyfriend. I made the call.

She Said…

I swear I have buzzard luck. Of all the times in the world Rico would call now. I was shaking in my boots when I felt my phone vibrate. You know how you already know who it is and it is the wrong time for that person to be calling. Yeah, just like that. I looked Ken in his eyes trying to search for any hint of fakeness. All I saw was genuine concern and sincerity. I kissed his lips and pressed talk on my phone.

"Hey Rico," I answered as I sat down on the chaise.

"Hey baby. I was expecting you to call me when you got back from your trip. How was the trip? Is everything alright?" he asked.

I could hear the concern in his voice and I felt like a complete ass. It wasn't in my nature to hurt people and Rico was no exception. He was a casualty of love, in the wrong place at the wrong time. Ken didn't make the situation any easier staring in my face.

"My trip was fine. And no, everything is not alright. I told you before that we needed to talk Rico. This can't go any further. I'm so sorry. I still love Kenyon. I never stopped. I feel terrible about what happened between us. It should have never happened."

"I figured you were going to say this. That's one thing I learned while I was with you that you're an honorable person. There were times when your body may have been there with me but your mind was somewhere else. I wanted to believe that you were in love with me but I knew you still loved him. I can't say I'm happy but I can deal with it. You're a cool ass chick Koi. There's something else I wanted to tell you though, it's about…"

My line clicked and I saw that it was Nika. It was her second time calling so I interrupted him to answer the line.

"What's up Nika?"

"Are you going to be ready? I'll be by there in a half an hour," screamed Nika.

"Why are you yelling? No, I'm not ready. I don't think I'm hanging. I told you I was tired earlier plus I'm over Ken's parents' house and I'll probably be here for a minute. You go on without me tonight."

"What the hell are you doing over there? Girl, you ain't learned your lesson yet? That nigga is no good; whatever he's trying to feed you is a lie. When are you going to wake up and see that? Don't listen to shit he says."

I heard my line click indicating that Rico had hung up on the other line. But then it registered to me that I hadn't told Nika that Ken was there with me. I flashed back to the conversation that Chyna and I had yesterday. Something was up with Nika and I intended on finding out exactly what it was. But right now I had bigger things to focus on.

"Look, don't worry about me and Ken, Nika. Go out and do your thing. I'll talk to you tomorrow." I didn't even give her a chance to say shit else. I hung up and closed my cell phone.

"Your girl is a trip. I heard everything her big ass mouth was saying," said Ken.

"Don't worry about Nika. I don't know what her problem is but she definitely has one," I explained.

"So old boy was ok with you breaking it off?" he asked.

"I guess he was ok. In his defense baby, he is a hell of a worker and I actually would hate to lose him from my team. Let's talk more about this before we make any major moves." Sequoia couldn't help it, the business side of her always found a way to peek out. Rico was a valuable player on her team and she was almost positive they could find a way to work this out amicably.

"Baby, as long as you are back in my life. Nothing else really matters," said Ken as he stroked my hair and planted kisses on my face.

We sat in front of the fire and talked into the wee hours of the morning.

He Said…She Said

Chapter 27

He Said…

9'm having one of the best days of my life. Work is straight up great. All of my clients are happy, my sister is here, but the most important thing is I have been given the opportunity to get my soul mate back. Koi didn't say I could come home but we talked until the birds came up at my parents' house. And I got the feeling that her loft will soon be ours once again. I tried to call Colin and touch bases with him about last night but I kept getting his voice mail, which was weird. I left a message and figured he would call me back when he checked his voicemail. I was going to run over to Koi's office and take her to lunch but I had to call Tanisha to discuss some things in her portfolio plus I wanted to make sure all was well with her. She didn't deserve to be hurting either.

I buzzed Shanice. "Yes Mr. Burnett. What can I do for you?" she responded.

"Shanice, I need you to call and get my mom and sister the ultimate spa package at the Greenhouse on 57th. Send a car for them both and also get Ms. Roberts on the phone and bring me her file."

I had to admit that Shanice had done a 360. Memories of that one night still haunted me but she never even brought it up and all flirting had completely ceased. We have a completely all business relationship and she is good at what she does. Who am I kidding? She's been great for the last few weeks. She seems to have changed her whole attitude. It was time for her 90 day review and I am going to give her a raise but with everything that was going on with Koi, I haven't had a moment to think about anything but Koi.

She knocked once and came in. "Here's the file you asked me for and I've made the reservations for your mom and sister. I didn't call them though, because I thought it may sound better coming from you."

"Thanks. You're right. I'll call them but I need you to do one more thing for me."

"Sure. What's that?"

"Well first I want you to go to your desk and pack…"

"Mr. Burnett I can't afford to lose this job."

I laughed because that was definitely not the direction I was going. She was staring at me with tears in her eyes so I quickly continued my sentence.

"Shanice, I can't afford to lose you, so I need you to pack up your desk and call your mom or a friend and invite them to the Greenhouse with you. You ladies get the same package you got my mom and sister and take the week off with pay. We'll do your 90 day review when you get back, so enjoy your week off."

Shanice stood there with her hand covering her mouth. "Oh my God. Are you serious Ken? I mean Mr. Burnett." She had the biggest smile on her face you would've thought she hit the lottery.

"Serious as a heart attack. I want you to go and have a good time. I haven't been the best boss and I know it but if you could just accept my apology for all I have done. When you come back we are starting over new."

"I'm with that. Thank you so much. Now let me get out of here before you change your mind." She said jokingly.

"Before you leave call HR and have them send me a temp up here for the week you're gone. Thanks again."

"No. Thank you."

I was feeling even better now. Every woman in my life is good.

Shanice buzzed me again. "Mr. Burnett, I have Ms. Roberts on the line for you."

I'd forgotten about her. Damn, "Okay thanks."

I took a deep breath and answered the call, "Hello, Tanisha. How are you?"

"I'm fine Ken. How about you?"

"All is well. I was calling to tell you that you made a huge profit this week and I needed some paperwork signed off by you. I will send them by a courier today, if that's ok."

"That great. I've learned not to expect any less of you Ken. If you don't mind me asking, how are you and Koi?

"We're working on it. How about Brea? How is she?"

"She's fine. She asked about you just the other day."

"That's good to know. Okay I have to go now but I will touch bases with you when I received the signed copy back."

"You do that. Bye."

That wasn't that bad. I guess it could have been a lot worse. I packed up my briefcase and headed to Koi's office. I decided to take a taxi because I wanted her to drive to the restaurant. When I arrived at the office her pit bull of a receptionist was at her post, surprisingly with a different attitude.

"Go right in Mr. Burnett." I figured Koi had updated her on our status. I smiled and walked into Koi's office and was greeted by a scene I really wasn't ready for. She and Rico were standing over a light board looking at some photos. I really don't think I can handle this.

Janee

I have the coolest brother in the world. Ken had sent a car for Mom and I to go to some upscale spa in the middle of the day. I called him to thank him but he had his phone turned off and he wasn't at his office. He and Koi were asleep in the family room when I got up to go jog. They were all cuddled up like they never wanted to let go. I assumed this meant they'd come to their senses. He must have been in a good mood because it's not like my brother to just leave work in the middle of the day. I'm really happy for them. They deserve one another and just like any other couple had to go through it to see that.

After my 3 mile jog I was looking forward to a massage so when Mom and I arrived at the Greenhouse Spa we were both blown away. We've been to some hot places but this place was off the charts. I wonder how he'd found this place. Knowing Ken, one of his clients is probably the owner. I swear that man knows everybody.

Mom was already getting her massage; I was in the changing room getting undressed for mine when I overheard two women talking. One lady with a hint of a Spanish accent was telling the other woman that her boss had paid for the two of them to come to the spa and also gave her the rest of the week off. I was thinking to myself "Damn, she has a cool ass boss."

She continued her story as I slipped out of my clothes. She was saying how bad she felt because she had initially been offered some money to go in and seduce him. But he already had a lot going on. She explained that some chick that he'd messed around with and eventually dumped was basically stalking him and he was trying to avoid his girlfriend from running into the psycho chick. My ears were completely perked up now because this story was starting to sound all too familiar.

Blabber mouth went on to say how his girlfriend showed up at the office one day when the psycho chick was there and broke it off with him. "His girlfriend is a big power player in the advertising business and also one of the senior partner's daughters. She even told me to watch my back because my job wasn't secure and for me to remember whose name was on the door. That was the best advice she could have given me because I need my job and I said fuck Nika because her ass don't work and can't understand the value of a job anyway."

I'm standing there in the buff with my mouth hanging open. "What the fuck is going on here?" I thought to myself but continued to listen as she explained further.

188

"You know, Nika's gold digging ass knows all the ballers and shot callers. She was telling me how fine Kenyon was and I should try to get pregnant by him because there was no doubt that he would try to get in my panties. She said if I had his baby I will have hit the gold mine. I feel like a damn fool having ever even considered any of this shit. Yes, he is fine but from the beginning he has been preaching about being trying to be right by his woman. I came close to seducing him one evening when he was working late, he asked me to retrieve a file and when I came back with it I was naked. We got all hot and heavy but he stopped and said he had to go. I feel like a complete idiot because he is such a cool ass boss and I was dumb as hell to go along with Nika's stupid ass plan."

My stomach was all in knots. I wanted to see who this bitch was and whup her ass but I didn't know if that would be the right move, especially with my Mom here. But I need to let my brother now what's going on. Who is this bitch Nika? The name sounds familiar. I have too many questions that need to be answered but first I have to see who this bitch is talking about my brother.

He Said…She Said

Chapter 28

She Said…

I was surprised to see Kenyon walking in my office. I'm sure the look on my face said it all. Not that anything was going on. Rico had just come into my office and we were going through a few pictures. I knew that he wanted to finish the conversation from last night but business came first. Then came my boyfriend walking in the door.

"Hey baby. Did I catch you at a bad time? Your pit bull, I mean receptionist told me to come in," said Ken walking over to me.

"No, you didn't. Rico and I were just going over some business and I think we've agreed on a few. So give me a minute Rico, and I'll come get you when I'm done here." I said trying to play it cool knowing I was shaking like a leaf on a breezy day.

"No problem boss lady," said Rico as he gave Ken the once over and walked out the door. He peeked his head back in and said, "Don't forget I still need to talk to you later."

I saw the uncomfortable look on Kenyon's face and completely understood. "Ok, I won't."

"Sorry about that. I didn't know you were coming over here. Are we doing lunch?" I asked hoping that he could get past what he's just seen. Much to my surprise he answered with no attitude at all.

"I was trying to surprise you. Surprise!" he said and grabbed me by the waist and kissed me. We fit like hand in glove. I was so happy that he was back in my life. Of course we would proceed with caution but I was happy to have him back. I grabbed my Gucci bag and told my assistant that I'd be back shortly.

He had taken a taxi over so we jumped into my car and tried to decide where we wanted to go. I had some salad fixings

191

at the loft that were probably about to go bad so I suggested we go home for salad.

Pulling into the parking structure with Kenyon felt weird. I couldn't imagine what he was feeling right now. I wished like hell I could replay that fateful day over. I would have never even gone to his office. From what he'd told me last night. He had been done dealing with that chick and she was basically stalking him. I know it sounds really crazy but I believe him. I saw the conniving look in her eye mixed with desperation when I went in his office. I could definitely see her stalking him. Of course that doesn't excuse the fact that he was dealing with her in the first place but I'd agreed to let that wound heal. It was going to definitely be a process but we were both committed to trying.

If I could do it all over again. I would have let him handle it. He told me there was a lot that he had to tell me. I just hoped it wasn't anything worse than what he'd already told me.

When I pulled the gate up on the elevator Kenyon entered the house like a guest. He waited until I'd pulled the gate down before he proceeded into the loft. I touched his hand and said, "Lighten up baby. You act like you've never been here before."

He laughed but I could tell he was uncomfortable. He took a seat at the island in the kitchen and was staring at me as I pulled the lettuce and stuff out of the fridge.

"What?" I asked.

"Nothing."

"Why are you staring at me?"

"I can't look at my girl?"

"I didn't say that, but I know something is wrong. Let's talk about it," I urged him.

"Has he been here?"

"Is that what's been bothering you?"

"I just want to know Sequoia."

"No, I've never let him come here. Even though you and I were not together, this loft is a sacred place to me. We built this together. Every picture, every light fixture, we did together and I couldn't bring myself to bring another man here."

He came around the island and held me close from behind. I continued to cut up the vegetables for our salads. We both were deep in thought when my cell phone rang.

I fished through my purse to find it and saw it was the office calling.

I answered, "Sequoia Johnson speaking."

"Sequoia, Mr. Martin from the Fusion design company left a message that I thought you might want right away. They want the Reed agency to bid on the Ford Motor Company 2nd quarter ad campaign. The ads, commercial and incentives programs will all be taking place in Jamaica. I know this is a big one so I decided to call you instead of waiting for you to get back," exclaimed Phyllis, my assistant.

My heart was beating a mile a minute. My first thought was to scrap the salads and get my ass back to work to get started on some numbers. Then I looked over at Ken who was waiting patiently for me to close my conversation. "Thanks Phyllis. I appreciate you for being proactive. I will be back in the office in about two hours. Hold all my calls until then."

I closed my cell phone and went around to where he was sitting on one of the bar stools and started untying his tie and taking his shirt off.

"You sure you got time for this?" he asked kind of surprised by my actions.

"I'll always have time for you baby. I have to take care of the important things first and then I'll handle that." I continued to undress him and kneeled before him and took care of my man something proper!

193

He Said…She Said

Chapter 29

He Said…

9 felt like a ton of bricks had fallen on me when I walked in Koi's office and saw her with Rico. It was really innocent on her part but he was sizing her up, all while they were standing there. I wanted to say something so bad, but I knew that the calm and collected Kenyon would get Koi back not the hot-headed Ken. I couldn't afford to do or say anything wrong, but when that bitch popped his head back in and said, "Remember I still have to talk to you later," I gritted my teeth and made a mental note that I'm going to have to break this boy's spirits before he gets too full of himself.

Back at the loft, Koi made love to me so good. I could tell she was trying to really put it on me; my only hope was that it wasn't because she was thinking about him. Was she making love to me and thinking of him? Shit, did he do the things to her that I thought I was the only man that would? Did he hit her from behind? Damn I have to stop this I can't worry about them. I just really wonder if he was fucking her while we were still together. What was it about him that made her choose him?

"Ken stop doing this to yourself man. Boss up, fuck that nigga. You got you girl back just get over it." I smiled to myself and thought, "Damn that's what Lavon would've said."

Now that Koi was gone back to work I had to decide what I was going to do with the rest of my day. I called my office and had them send me a car to take me back to the office I needed to get my truck plus I wanted to grab a few files from the office. Once I arrived at my office I noticed there were two messages from Janee and one from my mom. I would call them once I got home. I just wanted to get back to my place and take a shower and call Colin and tell him the good news about me and Koi. He'd been so supportive when I was going through it, I'm sure he would want to know what was going on.

Janee

I've been calling Kenyon all damn day to tell him what happened at the spa but he's been M.I.A. What am I going to do? I figured I would just shoot over to his place. I hated going into Manhattan this time of day, it's always crazy but down right maddening during rush hour.

I hadn't been to his new place so when I pulled up I thought, "Damn my big brother is really on top of his game. A lot of celebrities live in this same building." I knew he was doing his thing and doing it well. The doorman opened the door I walked to the front desk and asked for Kenyon Burnett. The guy at the desk fucked me up when he asked for my I.D. and looked at some list and just gave me a key and the apartment number and said go up.

I walked into the spacious apartment and knew Ken lived here alone. There wasn't a hint of a woman living here. There was gray furniture with a big 50 inch plasma on the wall no flowers, no nothing that a woman would have put in here. The place was nice but I loved the loft a lot more. I started to make myself at home when I heard some keys turning in the lock. "Ken, I'm in the kitchen."

"John at the front desk already told me you were up here."

"Really? You have a list of people you give a key too?"

"Only you guys and Koi. But I knew she wouldn't ever use it because she hasn't ever been here."

"I can tell. This room is filled with testosterone." I said trying not to laugh.

"Well I live here alone. I just need a bed and TV."

"I see that and all you have in you fridge is beer and chicken."

"See you didn't look very well it is some turkey burgers in there too." He said cracking one of his corny ass jokes.

"Ok but I didn't come over here to talk to you about all that. Do you have some Spanish chick working for you?"

"Yea, Shanice my assistant. Why what's up?"

"Well while I was changing my clothes at the spa. I over heard her talking about her boss that paid for her and her friend's time at the spa."

"Okay and I always take care of the people that work for me. What's going on? I know you didn't come here to ask me that J. What's up?"

"Well I overheard her say she tried to seduce you for a friend of hers. She was like she was going to fuck you and get pregnant and hit you for as much child support as she could."

"WHAT! She was doing what for a friend?"

"Going to get preg…"

"I heard that part. Who is her friend? I don't think I know anyone that she knows," Ken said scratching his head and looking rather pale.

"Well she said it was some girl name Nika."

"Nika? That's Koi's best friend. You've got to be kidding me. I knew something was up."

"What you mean?"

"When she first started working there, she threw the pussy at me and I turned her down."

"Yea right Ken. You didn't fuck her? That's not like you."

"No J. I didn't. Lord knows it was hard but I really love Koi. Man, I was trying to be a good man sis, that's my word."

"Well her word is you two got all hot and heavy and Nika is the reason why."

"Damn, I don't think Nika would pull some shit like that. I know she doesn't like me but I don't think she would do that to Koi."

"Well big bro I think you need to find out quick, because that bitch is playing for keeps."

"Look I have to make a run. Don't tell Koi about this. I need to find out what the fuck is going on. I will see you later leave the key with John."

"Okay Ken. I love you. Don't do anything stupid."

He Said…

I don't know what the fuck is going on but I had to put the clues together and I had to do it fast. Why would Nika be trying to destroy my relationship with Koi? I remember once she wanted me but damn she knew how much I loved her girl.

I checked my Rolex and noticed it was a little after 7 pm, and I started wondering about everything that had happened to me since Shanice had been working there. First she came in my office butt ass naked, next she was there when Kim crazy ass came up there. Shit how did Kim even know where my office was? I never told her. She thought I worked in Jersey. I never told her I worked in the city. And how did she know where I lived? I only had one choice. I had to run over to this crazy ass bitch's place and get some answers.

When I pulled up to her place, I noticed Colin's car was there. I parked across and down the street. This was no coincidence that his car was here. They weren't friends. What is going on?

Colin's ass has been acting funny but fucking with Kim? I don't think so. I watched her house closely. My eyes had to be playing tricks on me. I saw three people I would've never thought I would see together walk out of Kim's house. Plain as day, Bianca, Colin and Nika all walked out of Kim's place.

I needed to get some answers and there was only one person I hoped wasn't in on this, Tanisha. I hope she could be some kind of link since she does know Nika and me.

My cell phone rang. I looked at my caller ID and saw
Wifey come up on the screen and still couldn't crack a smile. I
couldn't smile because I knew that the two people that called
themselves our best friends were really trying to break us up. I
had to put the puzzle together.

"Hello? Hey baby what's good?" Koi asked.

"Nothing baby. I'm just handling a few things."

"Are you coming to the loft tonight?"

"I really don't know, but I do have to talk to you. So I'll
call you a little later okay?"

"Well do you even know what you want to eat for dinner?
Baby, what's wrong? I hear something not right in your voice?"

"Everything is good. I just got some files mixed up but I
will call you as soon as I'm done. But I don't know what time
that will be."

"Well okay. I will see you later right?"

"Yea, baby. I'll call you when I'm done. I love you
okay."

"I love you too. Bye"

I couldn't tell her about her girl yet. I had to see what the
fuck was going on first. I just couldn't hurt her like that without
the proof in hand to show her. Nika isn't her best friend. I can't
believe she would do this to her. I'm really fucked up by all of
this, but I know Tanisha will be honest with me. So my next stop
is to her place. I can see it now. It's going to be hell to pay for
whoever is trying to fuck up my relationship with Koi.

She Said…

I don't know what was wrong with Kenyon but I could
hear it all in his voice. Something was up. I just prayed he wasn't
on some bullshit. I was committed to making things work but I
don't think I can stand more heartbreak from him. I put all the
negativity behind me and dove into my work. Then I

remembered that Rico had said he needed to talk to me. I buzzed the phone on his desk and told him if he had time he could comeback to my office.

He knocked about five minutes later. I told him to have a seat.

"Koi, I know the past week has been pretty crazy with all that was going on here and personally for the both of us but I wanted to reiterate that what we had was not just a fling to me. I was really digging you. I respect the decision that you made to try to work it out with your dude but I can't say I'm happy about it. But I knew going in that you weren't over him. So I take part of the blame. But I need to tell you who else we can blame."

I was confused. Who else could we blame for basically starting an affair that should have never begun for business and personal reasons? I let him finish.

"When I first started here all I knew about you was your stellar reputation in the advertising industry. I was staying with Chanelle because I'd just broken up with my girlfriend of five years. She'd put me out and Chanelle let me move in with her until I found a place.

Ok, so now the brotha is going to flip the script and say he never really cared about me. I was just a rebound as well. That's cool with me. It'll be easier for him to get past this whole thing. Maybe the girlfriend would take him back. I didn't interrupt though, he continued on.

"Well when I told Chanelle who I was working under she wasn't impressed. She said she'd been out with you and your man and Colin a few times and you seemed bourgeois and standoffish and she didn't particularly care for you."

That hood rat! She didn't like me because she is complete trash. We'd gone out to Mr. Chow's for dinner and everyone knows Mr. Chow's is an upscale restaurant. Why did this heffa have on a lime green "move something" dress on that looked like something she'd pulled out of a Luke video? And dumb ass

Colin could barely keep the drool in his mouth all during dinner. I was embarrassed as was Ken. Hell no, I wasn't associating myself with this video hoe look-alike. Ok, I'm getting pissed but I'll let him finish.

"So I guess she mentioned to Colin that I was working with you and a few days later they approached me on some bullshit. They wanted me to come to work and try to seduce you. I was supposed to seduce you and help break you up from your boyfriend."

"What!! Why would they? Why would you? Ok, let me regroup and get this straight. Why would Colin and Chanelle want to break me and Ken up? Colin is Kenyon's best friend. And Rico, you were playing me? All this time you were just playing me?"

"No, that's just it. When I saw you and started working with you, I fell in love with you. Their plan didn't mean shit to me anymore. Yes, I wanted you to break up with Ken but for my own personal reasons. I don't know what their deal is but I want you to be my woman."

"Are you out of your fucking mind? How dare you come in here and try to make it seem like you were innocent in all this? I fucking gave myself to you Rico. If you hadn't been playing this damn game I would still have my conscious in tact. I cheated on my man with you. Get the fuck out of my office." I screamed.

"I'm about to give Mr. Reed my resignation letter. I just wanted to let you know," he said.

"That's smartest thing you've said since you walked in the door." I turned my back to him and stared out into the New York skyline.

After I heard the door close, I broke down. I couldn't believe this. I had a million and one thoughts going through my head but the first thing I wanted to do was talk to Ken. I knew Colin was a snake in the grass but my man thought this nigga had his back. I still can't understand why he would want to do that

Kenyon. Maybe me, because he can't stand me and I can't stand him, but not Kenyon. They've been boys forever. I had to let my man know because he didn't have a clue.

I dialed his number and was shot straight to voicemail. Ok, now I'm getting pissed because I already know something is up and now he isn't answering the phone?

I hung up without leaving a message and called Nika's cell. The phone clicked on but she didn't say anything.

"Hello? Hello?" I repeated.

I don't think she knew that the call had connected. I heard talking. I thought I heard her say, "That was her stupid ass right there." But I had to be mistaken. I know she wasn't talking about me. But I wasn't mistaken when I heard a voice I was all too familiar with…Colin. Because she was moving around or maybe walking the signal kept going in and out so I could only catch bits and pieces of what he was saying. I heard, "Don't worry…get theirs…stick with…plan." Then I heard her laughing. Then the signal dropped and I was cut off. I was so mad I dialed right back and this bitch sent me to voicemail. Lord if somebody didn't answer the phone and tell me what the fuck was going on, everybody's ass is getting kicked.

What the hell were Colin and Nika doing together? This shit was getting too strange for me. I grabbed my jacket off the hook and grabbed my purse. I was going to get some answers from somewhere.

As I walked out of the office I saw Rico heading into Mr. Reed's office. Good for his ass.

He Said…

I arrived at Tanisha's place and sat in the truck for a minute to collect my thought. I had to have my game tight to get the info I needed. My cell phone was ringing again. "Shit, it's Koi. I can't talk to her right now. I'm going to have to talk to her later," I said out loud. I just shot her to voicemail. I knew that was really going to piss her off but I can't explain anything to her right now until I know what we are up against. I couldn't spill the beans just yet.

Okay Ken, take a deep breath. Count to ten. That's not working. That shit really doesn't work. What should I do? Damn man, get yourself together, go in there and ask her what you already know.

And that's what I did. I walked up the seven steps to her Brownstone and instead of ringing the door bell that was in plain site, I knocked on the door twice. And then the knocks became banging and the banging became ringing the door bell ten times in ten seconds. The calm, cool, collected Ken from 3 minutes ago was gone. She came to the door and I could hear her yelling, "Just a minute! Damn, I'm coming! Stop banging on my damn door!" The door swung open.

"What the hell is your problem? Ken what's going on? Are you okay?"

"Hell no I'm not okay. I want you to tell me the truth right now."

"What are you talking about? But first please bring your voice down."

"Why the fuck did you come into my life?" I said like I already knew everything.

"What? Ken I was referred to you. Remember?"

"So you're going to sit here and act like you weren't part of Nika's plan to break me and Koi up? You have a lot of nerve. I thought you were real."

"Nika? I've got nothing to do with you and Nika and whatever bull shit ya'll have going on."

"Mommy? Is everything okay?" her daughter asked as she peeked her head around the corner.

"Yes Brea. Everything is fine. Go back up to your room. I'm talking to Ken about something."

"Ken!" Labrea screamed running and jumping up into my arms. I had to calm down if I wanted to get anything out of this.

"Hey little lady how are you?"

"I'm okay. Why are you yelling at my mommy?"

"I am not yelling. We were just talking."

"Well you two stop being mean to each other."

"Okay. We'll stop being mean okay."

"Okay, I really miss you. I want you to come back and play me in the game okay?"

"Okay Brea I'll try."

"Labrea go ahead upstairs. Mommy will be up there soon. I just want to talk to Ken for a few more minutes okay?"

"Okay Mommy."

I was alone with Tanisha again and decided to take this another route.

"Ken if you're going to yell, then you need to leave or we can talk like two adults."

"I'm sorry. I didn't mean to come in here yelling but I'm really frustrated."

"Okay Ken, what do you want to know?"

"I want to know what's going on. Why did you help Nika try to break Koi and me up? She told Koi you paid her to hook you and I up."

I was lying through my teeth but I was fishing now. All those nights of watching Law and Order had trained me to know people hated being the blame for the plot if they weren't the one who really made it up.

"She told her what?" Tanisha said, seeming to lose a bit of the calmness she'd had minutes ago. "Why don't we go sit down in the living room? Would you like something to drink?"

"No, I'm good."

"Well I'm going to make me a drink and I'll explain everything to you. Go in there and have a seat."

I walked in her huge living room and sat there until she came back. I was able to really calm down and noticed she still had a picture of us when we went out on top of the fireplace.

She entered the room as silent as a panther. I was only alerted to her presence from the ice shaking in her glass.

"Ken look I'm really sorry but I want you to know I never wanted to hurt you. Believe it or not I wanted you more and more every time I was around you. Nika approached me one night at the Pure Club and said she knew a friend of mine that you had helped with her investments. She knew that I was just getting over my husband and played on that. She said that you were a womanizer and needed to be taught a lesson. She said I could help her do that and still let you make me a boatload of money. With the divorce and his cheating, I was all for it. She said that you hated her because you had hit on her before and she blew you off. But what type of guy tries to talk to his girlfriend's best friend? So I was in like Flynn. I knew it was wrong to even get involved and tried to get out of it several times. Especially after I met you and fell in love with you. But her ass is like a pit bull. Once she gets her fangs in you she won't let go. Then I found out she had Colin hook Koi and his girlfriend's cousin up and I started feeling better about that situation. I figured if she was with someone else then we could be together."

She paused to take a sip of her drink. I was steaming. I wanted to break something but I maintained my cool and listened to the bullshit coming out of her mouth.

"Ken, you might not believe me but Nika lied about everything. She suckered me into this shit. She's the ring leader and Colin is her puppet. Colin seems to think that you've been fucking his girlfriend. They both hate you two so much for their own sick reasons. She wants you and Sequoia to suffer, so watch your back. They are out to get you and they won't stop until it's done.

"So why did you help Tanisha? Why didn't you tell me?"

205

"Ken I fell in love with you. You were great with my daughter. I just wanted us to be happy but I noticed how unhappy you were without Koi. So I was willing to let you be with her because your happiness is all that mattered to me and that's the truth."

My head was spinning. It was all starting to make sense.

"Tanisha, I need you to do me a favor now."

"Anything. What is it?"

"I need you to get Nika and Colin to come out to the Pure club tomorrow night for my little get together."

"Okay I'll try, but why?"

"I will fill you in later but I have a lot of explaining to do. Call me at the office tomorrow. I'll be there for a half a day. I'm going to get the Remy Lounge so have everybody meet you there at about eleven. Cool?"

"Okay Ken I'll try. Ken I'm so sorry, I really do love you."

"I wish I could believe you."

"I understand."

I got up and walked out and never looking back. Now how am I going to explain this to Koi? Tomorrow is going to bring this to a head. I can't forget to invite Shanice's ass to the get together. I am going to show them all, they can't get shit past me. It's on now. I ended up at the loft, she was pissed but I laid it all out for her.

Chapter 30

She Said…

I wasn't too shocked when Kenyon came in and told me what Nika had done. First of all she had been acting pretty shady for a while, then the shit I overheard when I tried to call her. I was hurt because I really viewed this girl as my best friend. When he told me that she had tried to push up on him my blood was boiling. I was pissed that he waited until now to tell me but there was no time for us to be squabbling. We had a plan to formulate. The worst part was my best friend was teamed up with my arch enemy, Bianca. I don't know how I'm going to control myself. I want to beat them both down. But I had to have a clear head.

When I got to work Friday morning, Rico's desk was clear. I didn't ask any questions because I didn't care. He was a pawn in what seems to be a huge game but hell, so was I. I am an expert at my craft so I proceeded on, business as usual. We still were getting mass jobs in so I was busy as hell. But I had enough time to call up my "best friend" and invite her to lunch. We met at Trattoria Di Tribeca. It took everything in me not jump up from the table and beat the shit out of her sleazy ass but I held my composure.

"Hey Nika," I said putting on a smile.

"What's up Koi? You know you missed the bomb ass party the other night. Your boy was there," said Nika as she slid into her seat.

"Who?"

"Rico. Looking good as ever I might add. What's up with ya'll?" she asked as if she didn't already know.

"Oh that? That's over and done with. I'm back with my baby. I've been so wrapped up with him I haven't had time for anything else," I said watching her face for a reaction. There it was. The slightest frown flew across her lips but was gone in a millisecond. This bitch was good but not better than me. The thing is all this time, I never looked for anything with her because she is, or was, my best friend. I continued on.

"So what's been up with you? Who's your latest conquest? Trump?" I joked.

"Naw, his new wifey has his ass on lock. She ain't trying to go nowhere. Do you blame her?" she replied.

"So who have you been seeing?" I asked.

"Girl, you know me. I'm never bogged down by one man. I've got a few dudes here and there."

"Nika, when are you going to settle down? We ain't getting any younger. That's why I'm so glad I came to my senses and got back with Ken. You know he's my soul mate. I couldn't have found a better man. Yeah, he made a few mistakes but I'm past all that. I realized that those hoes were just trying to get at my man but he did what any man would do if a hoe threw herself at him. This separation has made him see the light so we've moved on." Again I watched her for a reaction. This time it wasn't disguised so well.

"Girl, don't be no fool for that nigga. Once a dog always a dog. You're my girl and I'm just looking out for you," she said.

"Are you ok Nika? Your cheeks are flaming red. Do you have a fever?" I reached over to put my hand on her forehead and she smacked my hand away.

"Damn, I'm just trying to see if you're warm."

"My bad. I gotta go," she said as she scooted her chair back and rose to leave.

"Damn we didn't even eat yet. You can't sit down for a minute and have lunch with your best friend? Well then at least meet me at the Pure club tonight. Ken and I are celebrating our reconciliation, ok?"

"Yeah, I'll be there," she said and turned to leave.

I yelled to her, "Nika I love you boo."

She kept walking.

I let out a deep breath and the waiter came up to the table with our food. He asked where my guest had gone. I told him, "She went to bury her head in the sand." I picked up my sandwich and laughed. He just looked at me and walked away.

"Yeah Nika. It's on! Don't mess with my money or my man."

He Said…She Said

Chapter 31

The Grand Finale…

Sequoia didn't seem the least bit surprised about what I told her was going on with Colin and Nika. She even arranged to hook up with Nika for lunch. Everything was going just as planned. All I had to do is get Colin there and it was on.

I wanted so badly for tonight to go on without a hitch. I was leaving at 1 pm and I had a lot to get done before then. HR had assigned me a temp secretary by the name of Lisa Hodges. She was a middle age white woman with glasses, kind of on the heavy side and seemed like she'd been doing this job for a long time. She was on the money on everything that I asked of her and almost seemed to know what I needed before I did. I heard from Peter in HR that she'd been with the company for about five years and knew her way around here really well.

I called up front and asked her to get Shanice on the phone for me and also to reserve the Remy lounge at the Pure club for tonight. I wanted tonight to be a night to remember.

She buzzed me before I could hang up the phone.

"Yes Lisa?"

"I have Shanice on the phone."

"Thanks what line is she on?"

"She's on line two and you have a Colin on line one."

"Okay tell Colin to hold for a second and I'll take Shanice first."

Here goes nothing. I pushed line two and went from there. "Hello."

"Hey boss what's going on? You need me to come back? Don't tell me that woman doesn't know what she's doing. I left notes everywhere."

"She's okay. I had her call you because I'm having a party at the Pure tonight. I have the Remy Lounge. I'm going to ask my girl to marry me and I want all of the people I care about to be there."

"What!! I'm there I can't believe you thought of me."

"You're family. I wouldn't have forgotten about you."

"You are so sweet. I will be there with bells on."

"Cool, be there around eleven."

"Will do, and tell that lady not to get to settled in behind my desk." She let out a light laugh.

"Don't worry about that. See you tonight."

"Thanks Kenyon and I'm so happy for you two."

"Thanks."

One down one to go. I pushed line one and it was on.

"Colin! What's going on tonight frat?"

"Shit, man I'm just kicking it with my little shorty. Why what you got going on?

"I'm asking Koi to marry me."

"Get the hell out. I didn't even know you two was really doing the damn thing for real. I thought it was going to be that see you in another life time sex. You know that good bye sex."

"Naw it wasn't. Man I'm going to spend the rest of my life with her. I love her more than I ever thought was possible. So can my best man be at the Pure tonight? I have the Remy Lounge and I want all my friends and family there to celebrate with me."

"Yea man I'm there. Is Nika coming?"

"I don't know. That's Koi girl. I really don't like that bitch."

"She's cool man. You don't have to call her a bitch."

"Why you taking up for that hoe?"

"I'm not. I just think you shouldn't be calling your future wife's best friend a bitch. I don't think Nika is going any where."

"Yea C, maybe you're right. It's best I try to get along with the hoe." I said that just to get at his punk ass because just as I figured, he got heated when I talked about her.

"Yea well, I'll see you tonight. Do you need me to bring anything?" he asked even though I know his ass was steaming.

"Not a thing. Just bring yourself and be ready to hit the mall tomorrow. We have to get ready for the wedding. I'm going to fly all of us to Jamaica on One Sky jets next week so we have a lot to do. Alright playboy? So I hope my best man will be ready."

"Yea K. I'll be ready man. I'm really happy for you."

"Thanks. I'll see you tonight. One"

"One."

We hung up and my plan was already falling into play. Now all I had to do was hope that they bring that bitch Bianca and we can get this shit out on the table. One thing for sure I'm whooping someone's ass tonight. Now I just had to call Mark, Tone and the rest of the crew because Colin's ass really cant be trusted.

I wrapped everything up and was on my way to my apartment. My clothes were still there and I hadn't move them because I'm thinking I'm gonna get my bride her dream house after all this bullshit is over with.

Time was flying by as I was getting ready for the night. I decided that my attire would be a pair of Apo Jeans and a Button up shirt with the pair of cufflinks Koi brought me back from her mini-vacation and a pair of wheat color Timbs. I was looking my usual self for what was going to be a very unusual night. I heard my phone vibrating and grabbed it off the counter. I looked at the name and smiled when I saw "Wifey." I flipped it up and heard the angelic voice on the other end,

"Hello?"

"Hey baby, aren't you supposed to be getting ready?" I asked her.

"I am. I just wanted you to know I love you and I want you to be on guard tonight okay? Don't put shit pass Colin and Nika."

"I won't baby. I'll be on my P's & Q's. Are you going to pick up Janee?"

"I picked her up earlier. I'll see you in a minute."

"Okay. Last thing did you ask Rico to come?"

"Nope, I haven't even spoken to him since he resigned."

"Well you need to do whatever you can to get him there. I want everyone there who tried to hurt us, so get on your job ma."

"I'll try. See you there and remember baby, be aware of what's going on around you tonight. I love you."

"I love you too."

Looking at myself in the mirror I looked like a ten and all I needed was the right cologne to make me smell the way I looked. I took out some Shogun my mom bought me for my birthday and blew a kiss to myself and was out the door.

Colin

This nigga has lost his mind if he thinks I'm going to be his best man. I'm going to do whatever it takes to ruin this nigga's life. After Ken told me about his get together tonight to ask Sequoia to marry him, I thought it was time to put my plan from a week ago into action. I'm going to have Bianca come to the club when Ken and his fiancé arrive and I'm sure that will fuck up his whole entire plan to ask that bitch to marry him.

I got all my ducks in a row. I called Nika and told her about the party but she informed me that Sequoia had already invited her and she was just about to call me which I knew was some bull shit because she'd been treating me like a step child for the last week. It wasn't a thing though, I had a back up plan I had started back messing Chanelle. Nothing serious but just something to do. When I got home I called her to ask her to come to the Pure because it was time for all this to come to a head. I know that damn Mark will be there and I want to see the look on his face when he sees me and her together. The next thing I had to do was get Bianca there. I had her staying with one of my friends from work and I know by now she's more than ready to bust Ken's ass. The crazy thing about her is Ken never hit her off but she wanted him to. They messed around but it wasn't anything serious, but she wanted him so bad when I approached her on helping me break them up last year she was with it. It was suppose to be a prank but I was like fuck him when I heard him bragging how he paid for the entire trip to Chicago and we weren't pulling our own weight. I was so tired of his bragging ass. I wanted to get back at him ever since that trip and then him fucking Chanelle was the final straw.

Now I had to get ready for tonight the only thing I had to do now was get in touch with Larry, a friend of mine that does security at the Pure. I wanted to make sure he would be at the door so I could take my pistol in there. I hated going out without my shit and I really didn't want to feel naked tonight knowing Ken was going to invite Mark.

She Said…

I have a strange feeling that this night is going to be a disaster. Yes, I'm mad as hell. Yes, I want revenge but I have a bad feeling about tonight. I almost feel like we should be the bigger person and let them know we are up on their plan and then just be done with them. But my man is hyped. He's determined to blow their shit up and in a big way. At first I was all amped and wanted to confront them too but Kenyon is usually not big on public confrontations and if I know Nika and Colin, this is not going to be a quiet discussion.

I'm a little worried about Kenyon because he's almost obsessed with this plan. I know how he feels but I've never seen him so intent on making sure everything goes as planned. Plus I saw the look in Colin's eyes at the game. He hates me and I hate him. I really don't trust him. Ken has told me some really wild stories about his temper so I'll just pray for the best.

I had picked Janee up earlier and she was running around the loft changing outfits every five minutes. She wanted to be extra fly for Club Pure which was understandable. This was most definitely the place to be in New York and you were bound to see just about any professional athlete, rapper, movie star or socialite up in there. I gave her free reign on my closet. I wasn't as enthused. I threw on a pair of Buffalo jeans and a crisp white wrap around shirt. I put on my Jimmy Choo's and accessorized to the max. I pinned my hair up in a spiky little up do and I was ready. I gave her another 10 minutes and we were out the door. I hoped like hell that Kenyon was on his toes tonight. He'd promised me he would be but I was still a bundle of nerves.

When we pulled up in front of Pure, the line for valet was around the corner. It was 11:15 and I'd hoped that Kenyon hadn't started the show without me. It took 15 minutes for them to finally take my keys. I knew the guy at the door so we didn't wait in the line and he didn't card Janee. I made my way through the crowd. We were getting stopped every few steps but I was trying to make it to the Remy Lounge. Janee was on cloud nine and I could see her head blowing up as she was getting all this play from the brothas in the club. I had to pull her away a few times and remind her why we were really here.

As I got closer to my destination I heard someone call my name. Janee and I both turned around to see Rico. I heard Janee say, "Damn," under her breath. Regardless to what had happened Rico was still fine as hell. My heart softened a bit, I regrouped and spoke. I was surprised to see him here because I'd actually forgotten to call him. I assumed it must have been Nika and Colin's doing. Instantly my heart hardened again.

"Sequoia, I just need to talk to you for one second," he pleaded.

"For what Rico? To tell me more lies? I don't need anything extra tonight, for real," I said as I walked away.

I stepped up the platform and entered the Remy Lounge and immediately was greeted by my supposed best friend. She even had the nerve to hug me. I introduced her to Janee and had to admit I was proud of Janee because she kept her cool. We kicked it for a minute as I looked around for Ken.

"Girl, it's hot up in here. I just saw your boy too. You must have been crazy to let that one go," she said referring to Rico. "Oh, my bad little sis," she said remembering that Janee was Ken's sister.

"Yeah, your bad," said Janee as she turned and walked away.

"She's a feisty little bitch, ain't she?" asked Nika.

"Chill out Nika. I'll be back, I'm going to find my man," said.

"You don't have to look far. Ain't that him standing at the bar with that bitch all in his face? One day you'll listen to your best friend," she gloated.

I looked in the direction she was pointing and sure enough Ken was at the bar and a girl was standing very close to him. The Lounge was actually pretty crowded with all of Ken's friends so I had to squeeze through a few people and stop to acknowledge his boys. I walked over to him and as I approached them he said, "Oh here she is. Hey baby, I was just telling Bianca all about you," said Kenyon as he pulled me into his arms. I tried my hardest to keep my cool because I had vowed to beat the hell out of this girl if I ever saw her. But I stayed with the plan. The girl was standing there with her face flame red with tears in her eyes. She turned to walk away and I noticed Nika who was standing off to the side with a very disappointed look on her face.

I saw Kenyon's face cloud over when Colin, Chanelle and Rico walked into the lounge together. Rico went to the other end of the bar but Colin and the hood rat came over to speak to us. I turned my back on them because I couldn't even look Colin in the face. My man on the other hand could have beat out Denzel for an Oscar because he was playing the happy best friend to the tee.

"What up C?" He gave him the "you my boy"- half hug half pound on the back. And he was really over exaggerating. I almost laughed. Colin pulled back from the hug looking crazy as hell. He had that same sinister look in his eyes and snapped me back to reality and to the seriousness of the situation.

"Chanelle that jumpsuit is hot, ma," Ken said as he grabbed her hand and turned her around as to get a full view. Again, I almost laughed because he knew damn well that dingy ass black full body suit from 1991 with lint balls between the thighs because it's too small was not hot. Again, I turned my back to them. I saw his secretary Shanice walk in with another girl. Yep, it was all falling in line.

As I turned I noticed a stunning woman, standing off to the side of the room. She was practically hidden behind a very tall guy who I assumed was a professional basketball player. As she sipped her drink we made eye contact and I think she smiled at me. Crazy as it sounds, it was comforting. I almost felt like she knew what I was going through and had sent a silent signal of support. I appreciated it and I smiled back.

I guess at that point Ken felt all the players in the production were now present so he asked the bartender to tap the side of the Cristal bottle to get everyone's attention. This wasn't part of the plan so I was as surprised as everyone else.

"As you all know, I've asked everyone here today because I have an announcement to make. I wanted everyone who I care for and everyone who I think cares for me to be here when I did this. For the past 4 years I've been with a phenomenal woman. You all know her and I'm sure can attest to her greatness but I don't think any of you knows the Sequoia Johnson I know."

I was like "Oh my God! I know he is not about to do this. Not right here and not right now." He was still going so I just listened.

"This woman has supported me in every endeavor, business and personal that I've ever pursued. She stuck in there with me when I made mistakes. Huge mistakes that almost cost me everything. She has been my woman, my confidante, my ride or die chick and my truest best friend. And it's because of these things that I know that Sequoia Nicole Johnson is the woman I want to spend the rest of my life with."

I was crying by now and I almost fainted when Ken got down on one knee. He pulled that famous robin egg blue box from his pocket and the whole room was in awe. When he pulled the tiny lid from atop the box I had to steady myself. This ring was gorgeous. It was my favorite cut, Princess and it had to be at least 5 carats. It was beautiful. The tears were flowing at a pretty good rate. Out the corner of my eye I saw Janee walking up closer with her parents and both my parents. So I had been duped as well.

"Sequoia will you spend the rest of your life with me? Will you be my wife?" asked Ken.

"Yes. Yes baby. I will!" I screamed. The crowd erupted in applause. I was so happy and busy hugging and kissing my husband to be that I didn't notice the girl that had been in his office coming our way.

"Cut the bullshit Ken. You are so fake. Listen bitch, I told you months ago that this nigga wasn't shit. I've been fucking him for months. What part of that don't you get? He don't give a damn about you or any other woman for that matter."

Ken and I both turned to her at the same time. We already knew she would be there so we both turned and laughed in her face. I noticed that all the pawns in the game had gathered around us.

219

"You know what Kim. The joke's on you bitch and all you other fake ass people who thought you could come between us," said Ken pointedly at Colin.

"Man, I thought you were my man. You so mutha fucking grimy it's pitiful. What the fuck were you thinking?"

Before he could answer I lit into Nika's ass. "And you bitch; you were so set on me leaving him alone because you wanted him and was pissed when he sent your ass away with your tail between your legs. You're a hoe Nika. You could never be me. You'll never have a job like mine, a home like mine or a husband like mine. Stay the fuck away from me and my man."

Then it was pure chaos. It seemed like everything going on around me was in slow motion. I felt like I was in a dream state as I looked around me.

My mother standing there in shock. She'd never heard either of us talk like that on top of the things she'd heard. My Dad, oddly enough, looked amused. The girl Bianca's sad ass was standing there crying while Colin stood there boiling over. He looked like he wanted to say something but he couldn't find the words. Janee jumped in the argument and lit into Kim. She was going at it and they were about to fight. The mystery woman that I'd seen standing by the ball player was now arguing with Nika and from the argument I realized she was Tanisha, the girl that Ken had been seeing while we were apart. Ken was basically firing Shanice and she was crying trying to explain that she'd backed out of the plan and was so sorry she hadn't told him.

I looked around me and watched everyone yelling, screaming and crying and I just wanted it all to be over but that's when I made eye contact with Colin. He was walking towards me at a fast pace. I saw him reach under his shirt and grab a gun. I stood there in shock wanting to scream but I was frozen. He smiled when he saw the fear in my face. It was then that I knew I was staring into the eyes of a devil. I watched as he raised the gun and aimed it right at me. As I closed my eyes and waited for death to ascend upon me I saw two figures jump between me and the gun. Then I heard the loud pop and felt the warm blood spatter on my face. Then everything went black.

He Said…She Said

Epilogue

*I*t had been months since the funeral and I was still getting over the whole thing. I'd floated through the days numb to the world. I couldn't attend the funeral because I felt totally responsible. Besides I didn't think his people wanted me there anyway.

As I pulled on my ivory silk slip dress and pinned the beautiful lily in my hair, I reminisced on some of the good times that we'd had. I know no matter what, that he would want me to be happy. With that thought in mind, I let the guilt go. I rose from the vanity in my room and left the beach cabana.

The sand moved through my pedicured toes as I walked down to the spot where my Dad stood waiting for me. It was beautiful day on the island of Negril, Jamaica. My Dad kissed me and walked me to my groom.

Kenyon stood there looking grand as ever in his white linen suit. I loved this man. When I thought it could have been him that took that bullet in the heart instead of Rico, the tears started flowing again. He was crying too. We'd been through a lot but to Ken this was one deal that he was going to close no matter what.

Ken had found closure at Colin's trial. He'd be in jail for the rest of his life. So many lives had been damaged because of jealousy and deceit and we'd vowed to never let anyone infiltrate our union ever again.

The sun was setting on a chapter of my life that I would like to forget but I was embarking on a new journey with my soul mate and we had the whole future ahead of us. Nothing or no one could stop us now.

THE END

He Said…She Said

Order Form

To place mail orders, please send an email to:

dennis@dennislreed.com

Price: All books are 14.95 + tax (MI sales tax 6%) = $15.85

Books ship within 2-3 days.

Book	**Qty**	**Price**
He Said She Said	_____	_____

Shipping and handling: add $1.85 _____
Total: _____

Shipping Information (required)

Name:_____
Address:_____
City:_____**State:**_____**Zip:**_____
Contact Number (optional):_____
Email:_____

Your support is appreciated!

www.dennislreed.com